Six Months in the Midwest

Darci Schummer

Acknowledgements

These stories have appeared in slightly different form in the following places:

"The Last Supper," *Bartleby Snopes*; "A Good Face," *Conclave: A Journal of Character*; "Nobody Moves in Winter," *The Diverse Arts Project*; "Pretty as a Penny," *Midwestern Gothic*; "The Newlyweds," *Paper Darts*; "The Leaving Kind," *Rattlesnake Valley Sampler*; "The Parade" and "The In-Between Girl," *Revolver*; "The Sailor," *Twin Cities Run Off*; and "The Driving Hour," *You Are Hear.*

For my teachers, for my students

TABLE OF CONTENTS

Six Months in the Midwest

Darci Schummer

PREFACE

After a late summer storm, Minneapolis was in a state of mild ache. Trees had fallen in the streets. Trees had fallen on houses, crashed into the roofs of Hondas, Chevys, and Fords. Carnage had befallen branches and shingles; streets and yards were lined with leaves and trash. In the city's Midwestern practicality, many of its residents thought simultaneously, *Well, it could have been worse.* Worse is only relative to the amount of tolerance a body has for bad, and so the ache spread throughout the city in varying intensities, which averaged—according to newscasters—as a mild ache.

As summer dwindled and finally disappeared, each night the news included a forecast wholly different from the weather. The city learned just how much it would hurt in the coming week. This hurt was usually mild, represented by a yellow as pale as early light. Here a death, here a divorce, here a layoff. But here a wedding, a birth, an A on a report card. Most often the city stayed balanced. Of course, there were pockets of green when some neighborhood had been especially fortunate. Likewise, there were sections that howled in red—especially in the dark heart of winter when parts of the city became so consumed with ache that the residents could not even imagine the budding of trees.

In the city's Midwestern pragmatism, its residents clung to this new forecast, shouldering themselves forward against all that was certain to happen in the coming days.

THE PARADE

Frankie knew his mother had cancer. But the winter he turned seven, his parents did not speak of her cancer anymore, and she began living in her bedroom, leaving Frankie to wonder what exactly had changed. Whatever it was that had changed worried him so much that instead of practicing his penmanship or playing with his trucks, he marched around their apartment, quietly searching for remnants of his mother: a derelict spoon with traces of her saliva, an idle towel still damp from her palms.

All he really knew was gleaned from his parents' nightly conversations, which were muffled by the blanket they put between the floor and the bottom of their bedroom door. Despite their efforts, he could still hear his father's low-tiered cadence and his mother's thin speech, which was littered with Polish, the language of her dead mother.

"He's too old now, Halinka," his father had said.

"Would you want to know?"

"I don't know. I don't know what's better."

"Ignorance is bliss, but at least it's bliss."

"Jesus, that's what you really think?"

"I don't know what I think. *Jestem zmęczona.*"

"I'm tired, too."

"We're all tired."

"Yes, we are all tired. He's tired, too."

"Then it's better, don't you think?"

"The waiting? The not knowing? Have you heard him pacing around? He paces. He's pacing for you."

The room quieted for a moment, except for some rustling of the sheets and creaking of the bed.

"Come here. *Kocham cię.* Let's not argue. I just don't want to argue, OK? I can't argue anymore."

"I'm sorry. We won't."

"*Kocham cię.* Say it, please?"

"*Kocham cię.*"

"I love you, too."

Then the room had gone silent, and Frankie was left wondering again, wondering what it was he did not know.

*

When Frankie's mother was well, they used to spend afternoons in downtown Minneapolis. Their last trip had been late that summer, August, when the afternoons stretched long and hot over the city and everyone soaked up as much warmth as they could because they knew that soon it would be gone. Had he known this was to be the last trip, he would have tried to remember it better, all the parts instead of just some of them. He remembered ambling with his mother through the streets that day, streets crowded with people in suits and skirts. His mother talked while they walked, as she always did, narrating their journey in a mixture of Polish and English. He remembered that nothing had seemed amiss.

"Do you remember what happens on this street?" she asked as they walked down Nicollet Mall.

"The parade?" he said, envisioning him, his mother, and his father bundled up and watching the floats while drinking hot cocoa and eating hot dogs.

"That's right. Are you already excited to see Santa this year?"

"Yes."

"I bet you are. I am, too." She paused, stopping to point their held hands at a tan, elegantly peaked structure on the skyline. "See that building? That's the Foshay. That used to be the tallest building in Minneapolis. Skyscraper. *Wieżowiec.* Can you say that? *Wieżowiec.* "

"*Wieżowiec,*" he repeated.

"Good. Again."

"*Wieżowiec.* "

"Now once more."

"*Wieżowiec.* "

"Remember, if you use a word three times, it's yours. There," she said, pointing at the Medical Arts Building. "Do you know who's in there?"

"Doctors."

"Right. *Lekarze.*"

"*Lekarze.* "

"Good! One more time, my *rybko,* my little fish."

"*Lekarze.* "

She had pulled him into a doorway then, out of the sidewalk's traffic, and leaned down close enough to his face so that he could smell the coconut shampoo she used.

"It's important that you keep practicing the words, OK, *rybko?* Don't forget. Grandma wanted me to know them, so I learned them. She would want you to know them, and I do, too." She touched the tip of her nose to the tip of his. "*Chodź,*" she said, signaling him to come along.

But then a teenage boy had approached them, blocking their path. He was tall and thin, his clothes crooked and dirty. Frankie thought there was something strange about his eyes, their winter blue core. They gave him the same feeling he got when he saw an empty bus drive by at night, the inside of it hollow and glowing.

4

"Do you have a quarter?" the boy asked. Frankie stared but did not respond, and so the teenager asked again, "Hey, do you have a quarter?" He bent over slightly, his vacant blue eyes fixed on Frankie's. "Do you have a quarter?"

Frankie's mother quickly stepped between them, pushing Frankie behind her back while still holding his hand. "I'm sorry," she said. But under her breath she mumbled, "*Spadaj*," a word Frankie knew she used when she was angry.

A few moments after they had passed him, Frankie turned and looked back, but the teenager was gone, disappeared into the cross-weaved threads of people. *Duch*, he thought, a word his mother had taught him on Halloween. *Ghost.*

*

Frankie's mother was in bed as hard afternoon light slanted through the living room window. His blue jeans were lit up in different geometries, and as he rocked back and forth, the shapes changed. He had not seen his mother for more than a couple hours in at least two days though he had quietly monitored her activity, listening to the television in her room switch through news, commercials, and old sitcoms. His father came home from work earlier than usual and went straight into the bedroom. Frankie stared at him expectantly when he came out.

"She's tired, Frankie. And I don't think she wants either of us to see her feeling so miserable."

"When is she going to feel better?"

Frankie's father lowered his head and rubbed his red eyes with his thumb and fingertip. "I don't know, Frankie, I don't know. But you need to think good thoughts for her." He bent down on one knee and Frankie could see the middle of his scalp where his hair had become thin enough that the sun could reach his skin. He put his hands on Frankie's shoulders. "That's exactly what she said. She said, 'Tell my *rybko* to think good and happy thoughts for me,'" his father said imitating his mother's pitch and donning a smile that faded as quickly as it had come. "Do you think you can do that, Frankie?"

"I just want to know when she's going to feel better."

"Depends how many good thoughts you can think."

Frankie nodded, taking on the responsibility.

"Let's go get milkshakes. What do you say?" his father said, again forcing a transient smile.

"Sure."

After, Frankie lay in bed listening to the soft sounds of his house, thinking as many good thoughts as he could. He thought the words *zdrowiej szybko* on a loop, words he knew from his mother writing them in cards to his grandmother when she was in the hospital. *Get Well Soon!* Then he thought the word *eat*, a word he was surprised he did not yet know in Polish. He wanted to get out of bed, to pull out the small Polish-English dictionary his mother kept in a drawer in the living room, but he could still hear his father watching Johnny Carson. So he kept running the words on a loop until dreaminess overtook him and he no longer thought in words but images, images of her, his mother. Always in his dreaminess, she was there wearing a yellow and black sundress, the one on which she affixed a bumblebee pin. *Bzzzzzz...bzzzzz, she said. Don't let the bee get you! The pszczoła is going to get you!* Then she grabbed him and tickled him and hugged him, which was the point where he always jerked awake, the dark of his room an open mouth that swallowed him whole.

The next day after school, Frankie tried to sit quietly in the living room and color a horse in his coloring book, but his hands began to tingle, and he felt that if he did not get up and move he would burst. He walked to the bathroom and washed and dried them and then washed and dried them again. As he turned the corner to go back, he ran into his mother. She was wearing her black bathrobe, and her cheeks were pallid and sallow. Although he had seen her just yesterday, today she looked different, smaller again. From the plate of uneaten food she carried, the bread dry and the eggs shiny and stiff, he knew she had once again refused a meal. Her whole face seemed to sag, the skin hanging like an oxford on an undersized hanger. She smiled and held out her hand to Frankie.

"*Rybko.*"

Her hand was cool and dry, and felt thinner somehow, each bone glowing through her skin. It seemed someone else's hand altogether.

"*Mamusia,*" he said, clinging to her legs so fiercely that both of them were surprised. His mother let out a small groan, her voice like a board that cried each time someone trod on it even lightly.

"Not quite so strong," she said.

He let go of her, his cheeks aflame with the embarrassment and guilt of his love. *Zdrowiej szybko,* he thought. She put down the plate and led him into the living room. She sat on the couch, adjusted the scarf tied around her head, and then patted the empty place next to her, all the while staring straight ahead.

"The holiday parade is running now," she said, but even as she spoke, her eyes remained hard-focused on some point across the room, eclipsed by dull clouds.

To Frankie, it did not seem like the parade should have started yet, for his parents had not put up a Christmas tree, nor had they spoken of presents, whose house they would go to for Christmas dinner, or Mass at Holy Cross. His mother had not played Christmas music around the house, not the holy loneliness of "Lulajże Jezuniu" nor the raucousness of "Who

6

Stole the Kishka?," a song that used to make his parents dance around the kitchen, his mother wearing a red apron, his father holding a can of beer.

"I want to see the mice on the float, the ones with the big ears," he said. "Can we go this year?"

"I don't know," she said. "It depends how I feel."

"Or there's the one with the snowman. The big snowman. I want to see—"

"I said it depends how I feel."

"You have to be getting better. You have to. You're always asleep."

"*Rybko*, what did I say?"

He looked down at his hands.

Then she quickly changed the subject. "Did you do your *praca domowa*?"

"What?"

"You know," she said, poking his ribs gently. "We learned this one,"

He tried and tried but could not remember what the words meant. He grew irritated. It was such a small thing she wanted from him. He shook his head.

"Homework," she said. "Repeat it with me: *praca domowa.*"

"*Praca domowa.*"

"Good. Three times and it's yours, don't forget. Three times. Now get your homework and show me. I want to see how your handwriting is coming along."

Frankie got up from the couch and ran to his room to get his lined notebook from his backpack. He had written in neatly angled cursive, knowing it pleased his mother, who prided herself on her own handwriting.

He hurried back to the living room, afraid she would be gone by the time he got there, but she wasn't.

"I wrote about you and dad."

"That's wonderful. Can you read it to me?" She leaned back and closed her eyes.

"Sure." Slowly and evenly, Frankie read his composition about going on a picnic with his parents the previous spring. It had been an unusually warm day around Easter, and they had eaten sandwiches and fed pigeons and squirrels. He remembered how warm it had been, how he had lain on his back and let the sun warm his face and his stomach while his parents' voices ebbed and flowed around him. He remembered being happy.

"*Piękny*, just *piękny*. Beautiful. I remember that day, too." With her eyes still closed, she reached her hand out and ran it over his paper. "Your writing feels even and neat," she said. "So grown up. Let's write something today, should we?"

Frankie nodded and smiled at her. It was what they did together since she had been sick. He handed her a piece of paper, a freshly sharpened pencil, and a book to lean on. He watched as she carefully wrote his name in perfect cursive.

"There," she said. "How do you like that?"

"I like it."

"Good. Your turn now. Can you write some of the new words we learned? How about *praca domowa?* I'll write it first and then you can try." She carefully scripted the letters, saying them aloud. "*P-r-a-c-a*, then a space, *d-o-m-o-w-a*."

After she was done, Frankie slowly began copying the letters onto his paper, while his mother continued writing, first his name, then his father's name, stopping after she committed a carefully shaped H to paper, the first letter of her own name.

"Let me see," his mother said, when he had finished. "No, this isn't right. You missed a letter. Find the letter you missed and start over again," she said with a new sharpness in her voice.

"I'm sorry. I didn't ..."

"Do it again," she said, with the same edge. "You have to practice."

Frankie began writing, this time his hand stiff under her watch.

"Now another," she said. "One you remember. I want you to do it on your own. You need to be able to do it on your own."

He tried to remember all the words she had told him when they were downtown, all the words she had taught him around the house, but his mind would not stay still long enough for a word to emerge.

Suddenly his mother swooped to face him, her eyes uncaged as she coupled her hands around his shoulders. She squeezed them, her fingertips plunging into his skin. "It's important. *Rozumiesz? Rozumiesz?* Do you understand?"

Frankie's body was stiff as his mother continued to hold him there. He could smell the light menthol of her breath and see a small drop of saliva tucked into the corner of mouth.

"Do you understand?" she said again, this time her voice softer.

He nodded his head, and she released him.

"Now write one word," she said. "One you remember."

Frankie's hand shook and he closed his eyes, fighting back tears, and tried to make one picture sit still in his mind. After a moment, it was the blue-eyed boy from the street who emerged, solitary and hungry looking. Slowly Frankie began forming the word, *d-u-c-h*.

When he finished, he looked at her and smiled. She said nothing, but seemed to retreat into herself so deeply that what remained next to him was filtered light, a Polaroid where his mother had been.

"Frankie, *jestem zmęczona*. Can you help me up?"

"But I never see you," he said.

"Let's not argue. I'm too tired."

"But—*Mamusia*, it's too soon to go back."

"I said I don't want to argue."

He stood up and intertwined his hands with hers. He leaned back with all his strength and pulled her towards him, so that his mother who felt as light as a hawk's feather, sprang up from the couch and said, "Thank you, *rybko*." She leaned down and kissed his cheek. "I love you. *Kocham cię*. Don't forget, *rybko*." Then she walked away and did not turn back toward him as she shut her bedroom door.

Silence fell on her room and a new brand of terror settled in Frankie. When he tried to imagine his mother and him together at the parade, he could not picture it happening, and it seemed that the days would pass as they had been passing without end, that nothing would get better. By the time his father came home, Frankie was angry. He did not feel like sitting across from his father in some restaurant or watching his father shop for another striped tie. He went into his bedroom, closed the door, and lay on his bed in the dark counting good thoughts until his father came and flipped on the light. He was holding a can of beer, his eyes warm and glassy.

"The parade is running tonight," he said.

"I know."

"Your mom asked if I would take you."

"But she said she might take me."

"She isn't feeling up to it."

"Can't we wait for her? Can't we go another night?"

"Frankie," his father paused, slowly turning the can of beer in his hand, "she asked me to take you tonight. We just have to do the best we can on our own, OK?"

"But, I don't want to go without her."

"I know. I don't want to either," his voice trailed. "I don't want to either."

In that moment, Frankie recognized a quality in his father's voice that he had heard in his mother's only that afternoon. He turned over and looked at his father's face. It was flush and blank and something else, something that Frankie didn't recognize, but something he knew meant his father needed him now.

"She gave me this money to give to you for hot chocolate. Here," his father said, putting a few crumpled dollars in his hand, "it's all from her." Then his father said something he rarely said and did something he rarely did. "*Kocham cię*," he said, leaning over and kissing Frankie on the top of his head.

*

That night Frankie and his father rode the 10-bus downtown. Hard cold had set in, and the city was locked in a glassy cell. The usual bus route he took with his mother had been changed for the parade, which meant they had to walk for what felt like a mile through the frozen maze of buildings and

9

parade-goers. Nicollet Mall, a street he had so frequently traveled, was barely recognizable. The air smelled like popcorn, like coffee, and the streets were dense with mothers and fathers carrying their babies and holding the hands of their young children who nibbled hot dogs or sipped hot chocolate. The whole Mall was awash with the night-muted brilliance of scarves, jackets, hats, and gloves, and when Frankie turned his head quickly, the colors changed like those in his kaleidoscope. Everyone was smiling, eating, drinking, or laughing, their mouths, eyes, and voices aligned in anticipation. "Cold enough for you?" they joked. "Gotta love Minnesota," they said. Frankie stared at them, at their eyes, which did not look like his mother's eyes, nor his eyes, nor his father's eyes, and his stomach whirled as his father led him by the wrist to the heated tents that housed bleachers facing the Mall.

"I have to use the can," his father said once they were in the tent, his face so close that Frankie could smell the beer on his breath. "Don't go anywhere, OK? Don't even move a muscle." Frankie's father tousled his hair, and then turned to a woman sitting with her children next to Frankie. "Can you keep an eye on him for a minute? I have to use the bathroom."

"No problem," the woman said, smiling.

Frankie's father turned and then Frankie watched him walk away, the hem of his tweed jacket swaying with his gait.

The woman who had been asked to watch him sat in the middle of a boy and a girl a little older than Frankie and when the little boy sneezed, the mother said, "Bless you," and kissed the top of his head, while patting the girl on the leg. Then they all dug their hands into a bag of warm popcorn, smiling and smiling. She offered some to Frankie, but he did not accept it. He did not want their popcorn, for he wanted his own mother and his own bag of popcorn. Soon the parade began with gasps from the wide-eyed spectators, but Frankie's eyes were not wide. He was not thinking of the lights and floats but of his mother all alone in that house on Jefferson Street Northeast, of how quiet it must be, and dark, too. His face burned. *Zdrowiej szybko, zdrowiej szybko, zdrowiej szybko,* he thought. Again, he could hardly bear to sit still. His whole body tingled and his mouth went dry. *Zdrowiej szybko,* he thought. As the seconds mounted, he felt as though his father had been gone for such a long time, forever really. The woman who was supposed to watch him was watching the parade, and so he stood and looked up and down the street but did not see his father. He stepped down one row and still did not see his father. Without any more thought, he charged out of the tent and into the street following the direction his father had gone.

He fought his way forward through the crowd, and the laughter and the talk, which at first had seemed joyous, now mocked him. Giant hands pushed food into giant, gaping mouths, and the babies, who had so recently been warm and content, shrieked as singing masked and costumed figures marched down the Mall. A troop of elves with lights strung on their green

10

pointed hats glared at him as they marched by. A bus topped with snowmen and strung with lights whose inside was as dark as a tomb growled past. Indistinct holiday music blared loudly, tinny in its artificial joy, and a ship with no captain loomed in the distance so large he thought it would overtake him. He felt lost, tangled in the light and sound. His heart pounded and tears begin to well up in his eyes. He looked to his right and to his left, in front of him and behind him, but he did not see his father anywhere.

Then from the middle of the fray, a familiar voice: "You got a quarter? You got a quarter?" It was the *duch,* standing directly in front of him, the *duch* his mother had protected him from when the weather was still warm. Frankie froze, staring into the ghost's blue eyes, which glowed in the streetlight. "You got a quarter? Hey, you—you got a quarter?" In his mind, Frankie saw the picture of his dead grandmother on top of the television and then the face of his mother, gaunt, the long, wheat-colored hair she had once so carefully washed, brushed, and styled, now half-gone and hidden behind a ratty scarf. For a moment he imagined they were both standing next to him, their hands perched like hawks on his shoulders.

"*Spadaj,*" he whispered, but the *duch's* expression remained fixed in its ghostliness. "*Spadaj,*" he said louder, and still the *duch* did not move. Then everything—the closed bedroom door, the plates of uneaten food, the smell of menthol—flooded him, and when he opened his mouth, the words, now undammed, rushed forth. "*Spadaj!*" he screamed. "*Spadaj!*"

As the parade-goers stopped talking and stared at him, he was sure he had yelled loudly enough so that his mother would hear him, so that his mother would know.

THE DRIVING HOUR

In the fervor of his courtship, Tom promised to take Meg to Cambria, California, the small central coast town where he lived until he was eighteen years old. He promised it in his usual way—grandiose, believing each syllable as it spilled from his mouth, though he had no idea how he would enact his plan. Now it is two years later, and with Meg's prodding and prodding from their friends Billy and June, Tom has finally pieced together a trip for the four of them. They are planning to leave within the hour, and Tom and Billy are waiting for the girls to finish readying themselves.

"Tom, we have everything, right?" Billy asks. "And plenty of …." He puts his index finger on his right nostril and inhales.

"Who do you think you're traveling with, my friend? Of course I have blow. Other than that, we'll only be gone a couple days, and we can always buy what we don't have," Tom says. "I'm just wondering what the fuck is taking those two girls so long."

"They are the fairer sex."

"Right. Fairer, as in *more fair*. Seems like a double entendre."

"So, I take it that you and Meg haven't really straightened out whatever happened at the CC Club the other night?"

"You know how the *fairer* are. They never get over anything. Meg's no different."

"What exactly happened anyway? June said you were talking to some other girl."

"I'm sure she said it with an eyebrow raised. Another double entendre."

Billy sighs. "Well?"

"I have to answer to you, too?" Tom shakes his head. "It was nothing. I was outside talking to this girl Karen and Meg flipped out."

"How do you know her?"

"She was in a couple of my philosophy classes at school."

"So why did Meg get so pissed about it?"

"Karen is truly a member of the *fairer sex*." He turns toward Billy, leaving a dramatic pause. "Do the math."

"Yeah, but nothing was going on, right?"

Tom turns from Billy toward the TV. A woman whirls across the screen, holding a bottle of shampoo, her blonde hair spinning out behind her. "We were just reminiscing," he says, keeping his eyes on the television. While at one time he had been, Billy is no longer Tom's confessor, not since Tom started dating Billy's girlfriend's best friend, Meg. Something changed between them then, something like liberty lost. Tom censors himself when he talks to Billy now, knowing that anything he says could get back to Meg. "Meg doesn't really let me out of her sight too often. So what do you think I'd be able to do?" he mutters.

"So something happened before."

"You automatically assume that?"

"That's usually why a girlfriend wouldn't let someone out of her sight."

"*Et tu*, Billy?" Tom says just as, thankfully, the girls come out of the bedroom. "Ladies, you look stunning. Shall we?" he says. "We have an epic journey before us."

"Let's have a bump before we go," Meg says.

"Anything for you, Nutmeg." Meg rolls her eyes. "What?" Tom says, cutting the lines of coke on Meg's glass coffee table. They all gather around the table, kneeling down over the glass. "Onward!" Tom says, inhaling the sting and wake of the drug, while he looks at the *National Geographic* magazine beneath, a jungle on the cover with a kid soldier in the corner, his gun alert at his side. The others follow suit, and soon all their hearts are fluttering.

"We're taking my car, aren't we?" Meg asks. "Tom?"

"Would you like for us to take your car, Nutmeg?"

"I already have a lot of music in there that everyone will like. My camera and everything is in there, too."

"Then your car it is." Tom says, feeling his jaw tighten. He knows there is a reason behind her willingness—not just music and photography. Music had always lived in her periphery, and photography—the reason Tom had initially been attracted to her—had become her dying art. Recently, she had settled for a job taking photographs at Sears. So, it is not what is already in her car that is behind her willingness, but that *they* would be in *her* car. She wants the power using her car affords her over the trip, the same reason she insists night after night that Tom stay at her apartment even when they have separate plans.

As they walk to the car, wind swirls around them and Tom shivers. Even after five years in Minnesota, the winter still shocks his system. He pulls up the hood on his jacket. There is little snow on the ground, but Minneapolis—as often it is in February—has been bitterly cold for the past week. Sub-zero windchills, dangerous temperatures.

"Colder than a witch's little titty out here," Tom says. "I need to get closer to the homeland. Keys, Nutmeg?" Meg throws the keys at him, and he catches them hard in the stomach. "Did you see that?" he says to June. "It's worse behind closed doors."

"Oh, Christ," June says, "Shut up and get in the car, California boy, before my little titties freeze off."

14

Tom and Billy sit up front and the girls sit in the back. The car starts hard but warms up quickly. Tom plays Thin Lizzy's album *Jailbreak* and turns up the volume. The whole car begins to sing.

Tonight there's gonna be a jailbreak somewhere in this town ....

The Honda races down 35W South. "The car bar is now open," Tom says. He takes a pull from a bottle of Phillips gin, and then passes it to the back seat. He moves in and out of lanes without using his blinker, as though the highway is his own little track and he must carry everyone through it safely. It is a performance—like his job, waiting tables at Palomino. He is good at what he does; he often comes home with a couple hundred dollars in tips after a busy evening. From spending a few years in the industry, he has learned how to play the customers. It is not hard to sense what kind of person they want; once he finds the personality they are looking for—silly and flirtatious or quiet and aloof—he adapts to it. It is a skill that can take him anywhere.

Tom has just put in the Loretta Lynn's *Country Music Hall of Fame* when June pokes her head between Tom and Billy's head rests.

"I have the perfect idea," June says. "Why don't we stop in Vegas?"

"Vegas? What would we do in Vegas?" Tom says.

"You should know. It was your idea a long time ago."

"The double wedding, Tom," Meg says.

"Yeah ... can't you imagine? It would be ridiculous. You, Meg, me, and Billy in a little stupid chapel with rented clothes and lots of champagne. It's just like we talked about."

"Brilliant, June. I'm sure you and Meg have been planning that for a while." His tone slips a little, but he cannot help it. They have all been trying to trap him for months, to pin him down to this plan or that plan.

Billy slaps the side of Tom's head gently. "June—you've always wanted a Vegas wedding haven't you, baby?"

"It's the only kind of wedding that I've wanted!"

"Well, there's no time like the present."

"Let's do it. I want to get to married by a fake Elvis wearing a white dress just like Marilyn Monroe wore when she stood on the vent. And I want pretty little panties with ruffles on the butt!"

"Then that you shall have it. Ruffled panties and all." There is a gin slur in Billy's voice; Tom cringes at his triteness. "Love you, baby," Billy says.

"I love you, too, Billy." June leans into the front seat, a piece of her dyed blonde hair hitting Tom's neck. Then she and Billy kiss long, their mouths making light sounds, their heads blocking Tom's view of Meg.

Tom says nothing, waiting tenuously for Meg to broach the subject. But she remains silent. He knows she is waiting for him to say something, anything that will bind them, but he has made up his mind not to give in to her.

When Billy and June finish kissing, he finally speaks. "Billy, let's have a little drink. Pass the bottle." He takes a swig of the gin. "To June and Billy," he says.

When the gin is passed around, everyone begins chattering lightly again, just as Tom had predicted. By the time they get to Vegas, he is sure that Meg will have forgotten all about June's wedding idea. For the next hour and a half, the car settles into a rhythm, alternating between narration and exclamation as Tom steals them farther and farther from home.

They maintain this comfortable pace until they cross the Iowa border. "Tom, I have to pee," Meg says.

"Yeah, I have to pee, too," June adds.

"All right, keep your eyes open for rest stops."

After driving a few more miles, Tom pulls off the interstate near Clear Lake, Iowa, and into the parking lot of a rest stop. The lights are on, but the lot is deserted except for one semi truck at the opposite end.

"I'll go in and wait for you guys," Billy offers. "You never know who could be hanging around here. Are you coming in, Tom?"

"Nah. I'm just going to stretch."

Billy and the girls walk away, and Tom leans up against the car, listening to the interstate. There are so many cars and Tom wonders where they are all going. He wishes he were in some other car, a car in which no one knew him quite so well, a car in which he had the freedom to be whomever he wanted. He unzips his coat and stretches, reaching his arms far above his head. Cold air rushes his damp armpits; he pulls the neck of his shirt away from his body. Then he stretches his fingertips toward his feet and a stream of air trickles down his neck and back. Its light touch reminds him of Karen, how outside the CC Club the week before, she had hugged him, her cold little fingers running along the back of his neck, their bodies fully pressed together. Her breasts were soft against his chest and her pelvis was flush against his. They were standing together the same way they had when they were lovers for a summer a few years ago. He let his hand go as low as the start of her ass and then his cock hardened so he stayed close to her for another moment. Finally, Karen began to pull away, and it was then that Meg appeared, her mouth open slightly. He had done his best to play it off normal, but it was obvious Meg was not convinced the encounter had been purely friendly. In the bathroom later that night, Tom hid Karen's number between pictures in his wallet where he was sure Meg wouldn't find it. He feels better now, knowing the number is safe, knowing he could call it and Karen would answer. He rests his thumb on the top of his wallet, the part that emerges from his denim pocket, thinking of the promise of Karen, thinking of all that possibility.

16

Tom gets in the car just as Meg walks out of the rest stop. She is shadowed and slight against the building. Small. For a moment, looking at her frame, he feels guilty.

She climbs in the back seat though there is no one in front.

"You weren't even going to say anything about it, were you?"

Tom exhales. He has expected this. "What did you want me to say?"

"I don't know. Just something, anything to acknowledge the situation. You always make me feel ignored. Just like a piece of crumpled up paper."

"Stop the theatrics."

She lights a cigarette, a habit he hates despite his own affinity for speed and gin. "It's embarrassing," she says.

"What's embarrassing? That I don't want to get married in Vegas? If anything, I think that's a credit to me as a person. I have standards that don't involve Elvis impersonators."

"But that's not … it's just—." Her voice is becoming thinner.

Tom rubs his face with his hands. "Just what? Say it."

"Do you even want me? I mean really. You didn't even acknowledge me in the car in front of our friends. We've been together longer than they have, and you don't even talk about marrying me. Then that shit outside of the CC Club, the way you were standing with that girl. Something was going on. You looked goddamn guilty when I walked out there. So how do you think I feel right now?"

"Can we just drop it, please? Can we just drop her? I dated her a couple years ago and that was it. There was nothing going on. What was I supposed to do? Not even talk to her?" He feels strange saying words that only have weight relative to his immediate position. When they are back in Minneapolis in her one-bedroom upper, he will no longer mean them in the same way.

"You both looked guilty."

"Meg, if you want to keep fucking talking about that, we can sit here all night. She's an old friend and that's it." He pauses. "Nothing happened," he says, emphasizing each syllable. "I'm not going to keep defending myself. The night is done and it's over. If you're that insecure, maybe it's your problem." He can hear her tears coming fast; her breathing is jagged. There are words he could string together to fix the situation, but he simply does not want to say them. He does not want to marry Meg, not in Vegas, and not ever. "What do you even want from me?"

"I want you to tell me you love me, Tom. Tell me right now." She touches his cheek. "Look at me while you say it. Tell me right now."

June and Billy are walking back toward the car. Tom sits quietly, watching them get closer.

"Tell me," she says. "Right now."

17

Tom holds his ground, though he knows he is making things worse. Billy and June are steps away from the car when he swallows and turns around.

"I love you, Tom, still after all this, I love you," she says, tears running into her mouth.

He can smell the remnants of a cigarette on her breath; he does not inhale for a second, refusing to take in the air she expels. In a moment, Billy and June will pull the car doors open. He does not want them to see him and Meg like this, not when he can't escape. "I love you, Meg," he says, the words burning all the way up his throat. "There? Are you happy now?"

The dome light flashes on and Billy gets in the car. Meg immediately turns her face toward the window. Tom starts the ignition. "How was the bathroom?" He feigns happiness, hoping June will not notice Meg's red face.

"Just fine. What did we miss?" June replies.

"Nothing," Meg says suddenly. "You didn't miss anything."

Tom pulls back on the highway, and the car settles into silence. The next couple of hours prove melancholy. The further south and west they travel, the terrain flattens. Tom plays Townes Van Zandt and Leonard Cohen. While Billy, June, and Meg are mollified by the music and landscape, Tom misses hills and valleys, the way they play hide-and-seek with trees, rocks, and cattle. Flatlands are too obvious, too easy.

"Hey Billy," he says, slapping Billy's knee with the back of his hand. "I need a bump. I'm getting tired." Billy pulls out what looks like a bullet and puts a small mound of cocaine on the corner of a credit card. Tom takes it and inhales deeply.

"Better?"

"Better," he says, putting on Iggy and the Stooges.

Slowly the girls come alive again. They begin giggling, passing the bottle of gin, and Billy turns back and forth from the front seat to the back laughing and joking with them. Tom grips the wheel, shifting around in his seat each time Meg's high-pitched laughter erupts. At the end of *Raw Power*, Meg leans into the front seat.

"Looks like the gas is low," she says. "I think we should take this exit." She is smoking another cigarette.

"This exit looks like we might have to drive a long way to find a station. The low fuel light isn't on yet—it can wait. We aren't far from Des Moines."

"It's my car, Tom. I know my car."

"I think we can wait a few miles. The car isn't just going to die."

"The fucking expert. As always," she whispers in his ear.

Tom grinds his teeth. She is snotty drunk now, and today after everything, he cannot handle it. He raises his voice, no longer caring that he and Meg are not alone. "I'm going to stop where and when I think the best fucking place is since I'm driving and you're drunk."

"All hail the driving Nazi," says Meg, laughing.

"Don't be a bitch."

"Whatever, Tom," Billy says, "It is her car."

"Don't say whatever. You sound like a fucking teenage girl. Do you trust my judgment or not, Billy?"

"Tom, I trust you, but it's Meg car. You're being an ass."

"June?" Tom asks, ignoring Billy.

"It's Meg's car. She knows it best."

The car goes silent as Tom steers them off the interstate and the onto a dark, two-lane highway, Highway 87. He looks back into the rearview mirror at Meg. Her head is turned toward the window, her lips pursed together. He glances back and forth between the road and the rearview.

"Watch the road," Billy snaps.

As Tom's eyes break from Meg's profile and move to the road, a deer runs from the left shoulder onto the pavement, a blur of tawny hide in the car's headlights. Tom slams on the breaks, swerving to the right, but even as he swerves, he knows the hit is imminent. The car slides on a patch of ice, and the left front side of it slams into the deer with a terrible thud. He can hear the girls screaming from the back seat and for a moment they are all suspended together just waiting for the car to stop, which it does, finally, after careening into the ditch. The force of it jolts them all, and Tom hears his neck crack loudly. For one perfect second everything is quiet, the headlights lighting up the edge of the snowy field in which they have landed.

"Jesus Christ!" Billy says.

Tom punches the steering wheel. "Fuck!" It is as if time lapsed for a second. "Motherfucker! Goddamn fucking bullshit!" He fumbles for the door handle, trying to get out, and then punches the door, the sound ringing through the car. He leans his head back against the headrest.

"Are you guys OK?" Billy asks, turning toward the girls.

"I want to get out," June says. "I want to get out of the car."

"Goddamn it," Meg says. From the tone of her voice, Tom can feel her eyes on the back of his head, blaming him for everything, along with the rest of them. His guts writhe.

Billy opens the door and pushes his seat up, "Come on, June. Come on and get out," he says, taking her by the hand. "It's all right, baby. We're all fine; it's OK."

Then Tom is alone with Meg; June and Billy's car doors slam in the highway darkness. He says nothing to her. He wants her to say something first. She must make the first move so that he knows how to respond. Politics, the structure of love.

19

He rubs his hand across his brow and her sobs start before she gets any words out. "I'm sorry, Tom. I shouldn't have said anything. I should have just let you drive. I'm so sorry."

The apology comes too easily, too cleanly. He doesn't trust it. "You're not sorry. You're happy. This is the kind of thing you wait for. You just wait for me to fuck up so you can be right."

Tom gets out, pushing his door open against the slope of the ditch. The ground is slippery and he stumbles, falls on one knee, and then takes the few steps up to the road. Meg stays in the car, and he does not turn to look at her through the glass.

"Shit, I'm sorry," Tom says. "It came out of nowhere. I didn't see it until it was right in front of the car."

June and Billy are quiet, but Billy does not look at Tom and June has her eyebrows set. He can feel the weight of their judgments and it makes him want to tell them to go fuck themselves and walk away. But he can't. He is stuck with them, stuck with the Honda in the ditch.

Meg finally makes her way out and stands next to June, taking her hand. They stand behind the car, staring at its dusty Minnesota license plate. Tom crosses the road and stands by a small, shrubby tree to take a piss. It is there amongst the shrubs that he finds the doe. Her nose is black and wet, a thin line of warm blood trails from it to the snow. Like tree branches, her long, lean legs stretch out from her heavy belly. Her breath is jagged, evidenced by the uneven movements of her stomach.

Tom hears Billy talking from across the highway. "I bet the car will still run. It doesn't look too bad—just a little banged up. Don't worry, Meg." The car starts. "Hear that, Tom?" he calls. "It started right up."

Footsteps come from behind and soon Meg is by his side. She inhales. "She's alive, Tom."

"I know."

"Oh, Tom," Meg says. She buries her face in his shoulder. "What are we going to do? Can we call someone? We can do something for her, can't we?"

Tom steps forward so she can no longer lean on him. "Great idea, Meg," he says, "Let's find someone to call. Maybe the cops." He turns back toward Billy and June. "Hey—Meg here says we should call someone. You know—like the fucking cops!"

Meg grabs the back of his jacket. "Tom, don't—I just—she's going to be here all alone."

"That's the way things work sometimes."

Billy and June walk over.

"Shit," Billy says. June goes to Meg and puts an arm around her shoulder.

20

"Don't look at it, Meg," she says, turning them both around and leading them back toward the Honda.

"The car's OK, Tom," Billy says, "Let's go." He starts to turn around, but Tom stays there. "Did you hear me, Tom? Let's just get out of here." He waits another moment, and then walks toward Meg and June.

Tom hears only two car doors slam. He is sure that Meg is still outside, waiting, watching. A picture of Karen flashes in his mind, and he thinks about how the world comes from sepia into color on the arm of someone new. He breathes in and out: now it will come up from where it has been gestating and he will not be able to deny it.

Tom kneels down near the doe. Her eyes are open, watery slits. He puts a knee on her flank and a hand around her muzzle, and then quickly twists her head away from her body, snapping her neck. A sigh of exertion barely escapes his lips. When the doe's stomach stops, he is free. He stands there for a moment, calm. There is only the occasional rustle of the wind through the trees. The world is blank and in the blankness, he thinks of nothing. He is roused back into the unfolded scene when Meg drops her purse on the ground. She is staring at him. She knows everything now, he thinks. He spits on the concrete, and then walks past her toward the car. June and Billy have climbed back out of the Honda and are staring at him.

Meg darts in front of him and pummels his chest with her small fists. "You son of a bitch! Motherfucking son of a bitch! How could you? How could you do that to her?" She pauses, clearing her throat. "Take us back. I want you to take us back, Tom. It's all ruined. I want to go back now."

He grits his teeth. "You can't ever really go back, Meg. You know that. There's no way to undo anything."

"Then just take me home. I just want to go home."

"Get in the car," he says.

Billy and Tom push the car out of the ditch. Billy sits in the back with June and Meg sits in front with Tom, as Tom drives them back north and east to where winter will continue for at least another six weeks.

THE SAILOR

Edward's unmooring evolved from something, but from what he does not know. He is simply adrift in the Minneapolis grid, riding concrete waves in beat-up running shoes, his socks emerging in tufts from the cracks on the tops and sides. Street signs float past him like driftwood, and each time he tries to control his course, the words on the signs become unreadable. He loses sight of landmarks as well—a McDonald's, a BP gas station—anything that would serve to orient him. It is exhausting.

He has divided his world into the known and unknown, with most things slipping into the unknown: the city, his life before the present heartbeat. Each moment of his day is composed of a feeling. Right now he is thirsty. He thinks about licking the blacktop or anything that would force him to produce saliva. *Salt's everywhere: there's some on the roads right now. Won't saltwater make you go crazy? Neurons? Something with the neurons? Can't you drink your own urine? How many times? Only so many and then you're dead.* Someone told him about drinking saltwater once, about drinking urine once. A student—he reaches for a name—a student who had been in the Navy. "First they shave your head," the student had written in an essay. "It's part of how they take away your individuality. Then you put on the uniform, ironed and buttoned up tight. You don't look like yourself anymore. You don't even recognize yourself anymore. You're just like the guy standing next to you, and he's just like the guy standing next to him. There's a whole row of you and another in front of you and another behind you." The student's face appears before Edward like a mirage. He sucks in his cheeks, which have thinned considerably, and pulls his tongue against the roof his mouth, swallowing what little saliva he gathers. Maybe if he thinks about drinking a big Coke. He can feel the cold can in his hands and more saliva fills his mouth. It helps for now.

His dirty jeans, discolored and heavy with early March freezing rain, start to dry when finally the sun comes out. The sun feels good, and its warmth anchors him; he remains in a patch of light between two trees. He raises his face to the sky and spots a billowing cumulus cloud. He closes his eyes; an image coming to him: *A ship on a wall—a red wall—and the sun hitting the gold on the sails. Light. It lit up the whole room. I felt like I could step aboard. Feet on the deck, the wind, the wind blowing in my face. Salty air. Like that old paddleboat cruise me and Loretta went on down the St. Croix. Just like that except we'd be on a big ship in the Atlantic. Step right into the picture. What else?* He remembers a stereo, a Joni Mitchell LP. *I had to pick up the needle. It didn't come up automatically. I had to do it myself. And Blue skipped—every time I walked across the room, it skipped. Creak, step,*

23

creak, step, skip, that one line, that one line, what was that one line? "Hell's not the hippest way to go ...." More details flood his mind: a black velvet couch, a hardwood floor, a patch of sunlight traveling across it, marking a circadian rhythm. When he thinks about the place, his stomach grows heavy, the constant clawing inside it ceasing.

More words from his student's writing surface. "You just wanted to go home. It didn't matter if you were in Hawaii or Spain or Ireland. You realized that every place just blends into the next place. The only place that really stands out is home. You just wanted to go home," his student had written. "I just wanted to go home."

A cloud like the belly of a ship floats across the sun. The warmth that had been drying his clothing becomes noticeably absent, and he shivers. It is time to move along. He begins floating again, movement worthy of sonata, and he feels buoyant. He sees concrete pillars, gargoyles, a great building in front of him. The building makes him feel reverent, as though it is an ancient church of some sort and he is a pilgrim. *Bring the palm branches. Usher me in.* Perhaps in it he can find answers, perhaps he can learn something by talking to someone, anyone: a nun, a priest, God. So he rushes toward it. *It's like I'm Job and I need to talk to God.* When he reaches the front door of the building, he tries to open it, but it is locked. He cups his hands and peeks through the glass doors. A man in a gray uniform is on the other side. The man stares at him, pointing to the right, and mouthing something, but Edward cannot follow the words. The man opens the door.

"If you want to get into the museum, you have to go the main entrance. These doors are only open in the summer," he says.

Edward shakes his head but says nothing.

"It's free," the man says, his eyes softening. "You would only have to pay for the exhibit upstairs." He pauses and smiles. "It's warm in here, and the regular collection is pretty all right, man."

"OK," is all Edward manages to say. He feels so much more inside himself, but somehow the words will not untangle themselves from one another, so he walks away. He turns left, wanders off down the street, and turns left again to walk down the long side of the building. There is a row of houses, some lovely, some in varying states of disrepair across the street. He stops in front of one that has a "For Sale" sign prominent in its yard. Then he feels the water surge, and he floats farther down the street until he meets another house, an empty house with a "No Trespassing" sign in the window. When he reaches it, his clothes are sucked tight to his body; all the water disappears. *What happened? No. What did I do? No. What have I done? No. No. No.* He can clearly picture the inside of that house, the room with records, the hardwood floors, the ship picture. *This was it. This was the house. And Loretta in the house. She was smiling and then not smiling; she was slamming cupboards; then she was slamming the bedroom door; then she was slamming the back door. It was so loud and then*

24

so quiet. Like the sky changed. Sea change. The whole house falling. He feels sick thinking of it all.

His student's voice comes to him again. "They hated you sometimes when you left, but you kept leaving. You cared, but this was bigger than you were. It was bigger than the both of you were. You told them that as many times as it took them to believe it. You called. You sent letters. You said whatever you had to say. You did whatever you had to do to keep them happy while you were gone."

Loretta, Edward thinks. *I was always thinking of her. What was it? Loretta, oh Loretta, what was it? What was it, Loretta? What did I do?* He closes his eyes, sinking beneath the water. Words and sentences divorced from their context, limbless soldiers, march through his mind.

I can't watch you lay around here for another goddamn day, Ed, smoking Camels and staring off like that. It's starting to depress me. You aren't the only unlucky bastard to lose his job. We're the new kids on the block. Last in, first out. You can't take it so personally.

Easy for you to say. You're doing just fine, Loretta.

This isn't a competition. You are so consumed that you aren't even here. You might as well be a sailor. Where are you, Ed? What port are you at and what native girl are you fucking?

Cute. I can see why you've been publishing so much.

Oh Christ, I'm sorry, Ed. I just don't know what to do. You aren't here. I don't care about any of it but that. I just can't pay the bills alone and we have to figure something out. I can talk to Bill. Do you want me to talk to Bill? There's got to be something for you—even just one class.

Jesus hell, Loretta, what do you think of me, anyway? I'm not interested in downward mobility and I'm no one's fucking charity case.

When Edward comes back up for air, he is seasick, suffering the acute nausea of anxiety. *Oh, my pretty redhead, did I leave you? Was it me all along? Did I leave you?* He passes the museum again and keeps walking until he reaches a park. "Washburn Fair Oaks Park," the sign at the entrance reads. There in the sun, Edward thinks the day cracks open like a crusted eye. *Clear as a mountain stream. Clear like crystal. These are clichés. By all ever-loving means, don't use expressions like these. Say that the day cracks open like a crusted eye. Say that the apartment sagged like a tired old aunt. Let go of reason.* He had been good with words, he remembers. He had known how to write and write well; he had known how to talk to people in ways they could understand.

Do it for the students, Ed. They love you. You have a gift. Let me just talk to Bill, Loretta had said.

For the first time in a long time, Edward tries forcing his mind to focus on one thing. He concentrates on stillness; he concentrates on silencing the waves around him. If he can discover one fact, one tiny thing, he thinks, he will understand the evolution he has been lost in all winter. Maybe he will be able to find some way home. The word is warm and round and he says it aloud. *Home. Home. Home.* He squeezes his temples with the heels of his hands, squinnys at the ground, and grits his teeth. *Think, you piece of shit, think.* After a minute, as the sun penetrates the shirt on his back, he takes a deep breath and a series of images plays in his mind, an old flipbook.

He and Loretta were standing there, staring at one another, still, tense. The sound of her breath resonated.

So, you've made your decision?

Responded to your ultimatum? Yes.

Jesus Christ. You can't turn things around in that head of yours, can you? You can't even see how I feel. It's been over a year, and we can't—we couldn't—afford the house. The house is gone, Ed.

Those are just threats. Don't be naive. They are only idle threats.

She threw a rubber-banded group of envelopes at him.

It's over, you fucking idiot. It's over. She started crying, and he heard her tears not as weeping but as a melody of his own making, beautiful, yet unmoving. She pummeled his chest with her fists. *It's over, it's all over, it's all over.* He remembered his shoulder dampening from a mixture of her saliva and tears. *Fuck you, Ed.* She put her arms around him, clung to him tightly. He remembered stretching his arms out, hovering over her, unable to clasp his hands together behind his back.

I'll pack my things.

I've already packed them. Where have you been this past week? Where have you been?

I've been pleasanter places. Seen things you haven't seen. Done things you haven't done. I have volumes.

Have you listened to yourself? You don't even make sense. Where are you going to go? You aren't coming with me. Not this time. Not anymore. Where are you going to go?

I'm just going to go out that door and start walking. Everything is on the other side of that door.

You need help. And I don't know what to do. I don't know how to help you.

I told you—I'm no one's fucking charity case. I don't need help.

Just remember, in the end, it's your pride that undid this. Nothing but stupid pride.

Then there was the brilliant green of her sweater as she walked away. The house was devoid of the sounds that had been his life.

As the last page of the flipbook turns, Edward begins to weep.

When the tears subside, he no longer feels like he is floating, but as though he's grounded. He takes a deep breath, unafraid of water filling his nostrils. *Washburn Fair Oaks. I know now.* He points in front of himself. *The sun rises there. East.* He points behind himself. *The sun sets here. West.* He points to his left. *Polaris rises here. North.* He points to his right. *Centaur, here. South.* A slight wind comes up and rushes through his hair, which has grown long. It feels like a wind born of land, not of sea, and he turns his face up to take it in. He walks east, and then turns north. Soon he is in front of a large building made of red stone. He is drawn towards it, but he cannot articulate his attraction: it too looks holy, reverent. He stands in front of it, feeling quiet all over, hoping that the warmth of the sun will never cease to shine on him. The door to the building, a big wooden door beneath stained-glass windows, opens and he swears he hears water part though now he can see that the concrete is dry.

"And when you finally stepped off that ship, it was amazing," his student had written. "You never understood the word 'grounded' until you got off that boat. You couldn't believe you were standing still. You couldn't even believe you were about to go home."

He feels like that just now, as if he has come back after being gone for a very long time.

The sun blocks his immediate view, but he feels a hand on his shoulder. *How long, Jesus, how long since someone touched me? I can't remember the last time somebody touched me.* The hand is attached to a body and soon he can see that the body is attached to a face and that face smiles at him, the second smile in one day. It makes him feels like a person. A tear slides down his cheek. The face looks like that of his student, and for a moment he swears it is his student, the sailor, but the voice that emerges from it is a woman's.

"Are you hungry?" she asks.

PRETTY AS A PENNY

When Mary walks into Sex World, her face and thighs, which had numbed in the Minneapolis cold, start itching as they thaw. She gives the stringy-haired clerk behind the counter her ID, then treads lightly across the black carpet, its pink and green party print reminding her that New Year's Eve is soon approaching. To her right sits *The Dollhouse* with its neon XXX sign, juxtaposed against a European-style roof with scalloped edges. Its three private show booths are dimly lit and empty. Near them is a giant bronze cock, saddled and awaiting riders. From the ceiling, mannequins wearing nothing but lace thongs hang like birds, their naked arms outstretched in erotic perfection. Below their watchful bodies, Mary begins circling the wire racks and wall displays. She runs her fingers over the tri-color packages and glossy magazines. Everything is plastic, dissected: pussy, asshole, tongue.

Finally, she chooses a simple blue vibrator. When she walks toward the counter to pay for it, the Dollhouse is no longer empty. The saloon doors to the middle booth are wide open, and a woman is perched on a red vinyl chair, a small tube of red lights illuminating her. Mary does not come to Sex World often, and this is the first time she has actually seen someone working the Dollhouse. The woman piques her curiosity, so Mary stops and fumbles with another vibrator, all the while furtively looking at her. The woman's hair is blonde and sharply bobbed—clearly a wig—and she wears a wife beater with a slit cut in the front. A blue string comes out of the tank top and ties around her neck. She is anyone and no one all at once. Mary has always been jealous of women with that sort of self-assuredness, the sort of courage that renders them fearless of becoming pariahs, for she has never been that kind of woman. She has always trod lightly through life.

The woman flashes a generous smile and waves at a man standing near Mary. He laughs a little but does not return her wave. Mary gets into line, where she is able to keep watching the woman. A minute later, the woman smiles and waves at the man in line in front of Mary. Then it is his turn to pay, and he darts toward the counter. When he moves, Mary is exposed, an animal in a pool of light, and the woman's eyes settle on her. Normally Mary would have turned away, but this time she does not, not quickly enough, and the woman waves and beckons to her. *Me?* Mary points at her own chest. The woman nods and then holds her hand up to her ear in the shape of a telephone, telling Mary to pick up the black phone on the front of the booth. For a second Mary thinks about just ignoring the woman, but she cannot— the Midwestern politeness so engrained in her prohibits it, so she walks to the booth.

Inside, a paper towel dispenser is mounted on the left above a black garbage can. On the other side is a machine that feeds on money with two signs: one that reads "$20 minimum" and another that reads "Talk to the girl before you put money in. NO REFUNDS." When Mary crosses its threshold, she feels she has entered yet another world again, part confessional, part cell. The phone looks like a prison phone, and the woman's face, like that of a convict, seems to say, *Don't leave. Stay here with me.* With trepidation, Mary picks up the phone.

"You don't want that one," the woman says. Mary forgets for a second that she has carried the vibrator past the "No Merchandise Beyond This Point" sign. "The different speeds stop working. I know from experience." She winks.

"Thanks," Mary says awkwardly, and then feels as though she should give the woman something, some small token for her advice, just as she might tip a waitress at a restaurant. She looks at the cash box, and then fumbles through her purse for bills, intending to leave the woman some singles.

"It's a $20 minimum, darlin'. Time's running."

Mary blushes, staring dumbly.

"Sign says it right there, darlin'," the woman says pointing to her right.

"I—I didn't mean to—," she starts, but the woman cuts her off.

"Now pull those doors shut behind you."

"I really don't—," she starts again, but again the woman cuts her off.

"Shifts get long when no one comes in, darlin'," she says in a voice that is all honey.

Mary's lips curl in a forced half-moon—angry that the woman trapped her here, angry that she did not stand up for herself.

"Tell me about yourself," the woman says. She has stretched her legs out and her feet are propped up in the corner of the booth. Now that she is closer, Mary can see that the woman is older than she originally thought. There are creases forming between her breasts. Light freckles litter her chest, and when the light hits her hands, the veins are thick, pillowy, and blue.

Mary looks down at the piece of plastic in her hands, a simple purchase she will make to avoid other transactions, and then sits down, her face level with the woman's. "What do you want to know?" Mary has always hated talking about herself.

"You can start with the usual stuff. Name, occupation."

"Mary. I work at Macy's."

"Sales associate in the burbs?"

"No, downtown, and I dress the mannequins."

"Wow—that's really cool. The front displays and everything? The Christmas displays?"

"Maybe someday—not this year, though."

"You'll get there, darlin'. It sounds like you have a good thing going."

Mary's face is straining. *If you only knew,* she thinks. As always happens, she can see an image of her feet in her mind, the toes freshly painted and beginning to swell. A record skips in the background. *Oh the sisters of mercy … oh the sisters of mercy ….* For a moment, Mary considers telling the woman the one secret that hardly anyone knows and imagines the look on her face as it is loosed upon her. Her knee starts to ache—the physical manifestation of her secret—and she stretches her leg.

"What else?" The woman pulls her feet from the wall and puts them on the floor. She leans toward the glass.

"There isn't much else I guess." The same knee begins a hot pulse, and she runs her fingertips down it until her kneecap is in her palm.

The woman throws her head back and laughs. "That's a damn lie."

Mary can no longer keep her face locked, so she lets the corners of her mouth fall, her brow furrowing.

"What about you?"

"Now, I don't get paid to talk about myself," she says. Her smile is coy. "C'mon. Don't be shy. People tell me all sorts of stuff. I don't kiss and tell. Professional courtesy."

"Are you a therapist or something?"

"I like to think of myself like that. Or just someone who is good at keeping secrets."

"Listen, I have things to do. I really need to …"

"C'mon, darlin'. Twenty minutes isn't going to throw off your whole day. I promise."

Mary stands. "Seriously, I don't have anything …"

But then the woman stands up on her chair, towers over Mary, and cuts her off. "Sit," she barks.

Startled, Mary sits. *Twenty minutes—I can stand anything for twenty minutes,* she thinks. It does remind her of therapy. She had been forced to sit through therapy before and had hated every second of it. The self-help books. The relaxation techniques. The questionnaires about her moods and feelings, her sine and cosine waves of anxiety and depression. The plans for self-improvement. It was all bullshit. Even thinking about it makes her angry. This woman trying to pull some trite piece of gossip from her makes her angry. Mary is tempted to give her something to hold onto. She inhales sharply; the secret has reached her throat.

Through all the nights that had become barren desert roads with ravenous creatures gathered at the edges, through all the vodka-soaked sunrises, she had said nothing to anyone about what was happening to her. As the creatures lunged, snapped, and barked at her, she had simply found ways to avoid her friends, ways to avoid concern, and ways to avoid pity. But here, in near anonymity and under pressure, she is indignant.

"So, you want to know something about me, huh?" she spits out, feeling her pulse race. "I tried to hang myself in my living room a few months ago. I did it with a jump rope I had in an old box of stuff. Halfway through I kicked my legs and the hook came out from the ceiling. I fell and landed on my knee," she rubs her knee now, looking down at it apologetically as she has done ever since injuring it. "That the kind of secret you hear all the time?"

When she finishes, Mary searches the woman's face, waiting for it to assume shock or revulsion, but through the telling, her face did not change, and now she leans closer toward Mary, and runs a fingertip down the glass. "Well, that was a damn fool thing to do," she says, the phone wedged between her ear and her shoulder. "I hope you aren't thinking about that anymore."

The calmness of her reaction disarms Mary, and she can feel her anger dissipate as easily as the woman's finger slipped down the glass.

"No," Mary says. "I don't think I am."

"Good. A girl like you has too much going on to do that shit."

Mary almost starts laughing, thinking about the classes she stopped attending just short of a business degree, about the packaged dinners she microwaves every night, about the utter constipation she lives in. Still, it had been so long since someone said she had *so much going on*. Regardless of whether it was true, the fact that someone even thought it made Mary feel stronger.

From outside the booth, music plays, the singer moaning the name of his desire. *Nikki ... Oh Nikki ....* A man clears his throat.

"There's always something worth waking up for, darlin'. Don't forget it. Every day I pick one thing to get me out of bed." Mary nods slightly then looks down at her boots, studying the white rings of salt on the toes. "Hey now," the woman says softly. "Hey, look up at me, darlin'."

Mary looks at her and the woman leans so close to the glass that the receiver nearly touches it.

"There's always something worth waking up for." She pauses.

Mary nods.

"I'll tell you what," the woman says. "Why don't you come back and see me tomorrow, huh? You'll know I'm expecting you, and you won't let me down, will you darlin'?"

"Sure," Mary mumbles to pacify the woman.

"Good—I'll see you tomorrow, darlin'." The woman hangs up the phone, gives a low wave, and then stands up, leaving Mary below.

When she leaves the store, she does not intend to go back the next day, or ever, but that night as she lies sleepless in a tangle of low-thread-count sheets, she cannot stop thinking about the woman. She examines and re-examines the situation from every angle, trying to unearth what it is that makes her want to go back to Sex World the next day to put another twenty-dollar bill in the machine to be near the woman again.

At 3 a.m., she gets it. The woman draws something out of her that no one has ever been able to—the truth. And living in uninhibited truth is freedom.

At Sex World the next day, the stringy-haired clerk is working. He takes Mary's ID, looking her up and down thoroughly, flashing his small, yellow teeth through an oily smile. Mary hurries to the Dollhouse and finds the woman standing up in the center booth, examining her eyelashes in a pocket mirror, her hip a peninsula, her hand resting on its shores. Just seeing her boosts Mary's confidence.

Without turning toward Mary, the woman puts the phone to her ear. "Darlin', you're back," she says, the inflection in her voice teetering between the declarative and the interrogative.

"I was thinking about what you said yesterday."

The woman puts the phone between her ear and shoulder and reaches into a small black makeup bag. "Now what was that?" she says, pulling out a tube of mascara.

"About having something to get up for everyday."

"Uh-huh," she says. She carefully separates each of her lashes with the applicator.

"You're right."

"Uh-huh," the woman repeats.

Mary puts money in the box, and then the woman turns toward her, putting the makeup away. "Always trying to help," she says. She sits down, her face even with Mary's, and adjusts the loose, cutout neck of her *Lusty Lady* T-shirt revealing a red bra strap.

"It was good to know I was supposed to meet someone today."

"Knowing someone is expecting you makes you feel like you have some responsibility to the world."

"Yeah. It does."

"I don't think I asked you anything about yourself yesterday," Mary says.

"That's all right. I was interested in you."

"What's your name?"

The woman stretches her hand out in front of her, examining her fingernails. She brings her index fingernail to her mouth and bites down. "It's Penny," she says finally. "Pretty as a penny."

"I like it," Mary says. "It fits you."

"Thanks, darlin'. That's what everyone says." She stretches her other hand out and inspects each nail bed. "So, I have a question for you. Did you

33

tell anyone about what you did—you know, what you did to yourself in the apartment?"

"A couple friends."

"And?"

Mary considers how to answer the question. Was there an "and" anything? She had told a couple girlfriends at the CC Club a while after it happened, but instead of comforting her, they had immediately marked her. She could see it in their faces. They would not look at her the same anymore, not the next day, not ever. Instead of comforting or inquiring about what had happened that made her do this thing, they narrowed their eyes and began doling out advice. *Everyone wants something,* they said. *You have to find something to want,* they said. *What do you want?* they asked, calling an end to the evening before she could even gather her thoughts. *We'll call you tomorrow,* they said. However, as Mary predicted, not one of them called. She knew they already considered her dead weight, Mary the college dropout, Mary the lush, and her suicide attempt was an excuse for them to sever ties completely.

"I don't see them anymore."

"Why?"

"They don't call."

"They don't call you after all you've been through? Who are these girls? Who acts that way?" Penny's voice rises, and her tone changes almost as though she has forgotten that she is behind the glass and that Mary is a paying customer. But the question is rhetorical, and after a tense moment of silence, Penny's honey tone comes back. "You deserve better, darlin'. Don't forget that, OK? You deserve friends who listen to you and take care of you. That's what friends do."

In the glass, Mary sees her face reflected over Penny's. As she shifts right, the light changes and her face completely covers Penny's so that she can no longer see her own. "Do you want to get a drink with me tomorrow?" she asks.

"Now, darlin', I don't know. Why are you asking a girl-in-the-box out for a drink?"

"I told you about my friends."

"Everyone's got somebody. I bet you got somebody. At least one person. A sister or something?" Penny says.

Mary shakes her head. Her father and brother had left her and her mother for Paso Robles, California, long ago, her father imagining vineyards and wine, her brother in love with her father's vision. She had not heard from either one of them in years, and she did not allow herself to think of them anymore. Her mother lived alone in a dilapidated ranch-style house in Brooklyn Park. They did not see each other often, but for every birthday, her mother gave her tubes of eye creams, face washes, and foundations and found polite ways to criticize her appearance. Her mother did little else than cook and speculate as to whether or not her father and brother had finally made their fortune as vintners. Green wine bottles littered her kitchen, all of them Californian.

"No, there isn't anyone," Mary says.

Penny's face is a beacon of tenderness. She leans toward the glass again, her breasts bulging, and her thin stomach slightly slumped. "Come back tomorrow," she says. "We can go after my shift tomorrow." Their time expires, and Penny gives a low wave, exiting the booth.

On the way home, Mary feels better knowing that she will see Penny again tomorrow. The hard cold does not bother her nor does anything else. The city, which she has long thought of as dead, is suddenly vibrant. Even the Warehouse District with its industrial skeletons is ringing, vibrating with each step she takes.

After work, Crystal works her key in the lock of her apartment. The walls are hard white and bare. She takes off her black, high-heeled shoes and walks into the bathroom, pulling off her short blonde wig, revealing a mat of dark brown hair. A lone gray strand springs up from it. She glares at the wiry strand, then seizes it and pulls it out. Next, she peels off her faux eyelashes, her eyes shrinking, and the wrinkles beneath them becoming more prominent. *How much longer?* she wonders. She is already off the stage and behind the glass. She scrubs her face with water as hot as she can make it, her skin growing red and smooth. She pats it dry with a fresh white hand towel and applies wrinkle cream to her crow's feet, to her forehead, to the fine lines gathering around her mouth. She shuts her eyes, breathes out deeply, and then looks in the mirror: Crystal is gone.

Now it is Penny who sits in the high-rise apartment window. She is on the tenth floor, and below the cars and buses and people are all miniature versions of themselves. From her perch, she watches pairs and groups of people, their ruddy, happy faces, mocking and jeering her from below. *Everyone lives life alone,* she thinks as they walk away from her. Friends would lose track of each other or engage in disagreements that pried them apart. They would bear these trials heroically, flaunting their stories of slight to the next person they met at their job, their gym, their favorite bar. Couples would cease holding hands; men would cheat, and women would leave. Still they would hunger for each other; they would try again, meeting pathetically over plates of bland pasta, posturing and selling themselves, carefully selecting which details of their pasts to include in the conversation. It is all senseless to her.

She will not think about her much, but now Penny thinks of the woman who came in yesterday and today. She thinks of Mary. She remembers Mary's eyes. The eyes, surrounded by creamy, unlined skin, like those of a doe, wet and frightened as though even a hand placed gently upon the shoulder would startle her. The woman's eyes made Penny pity her, an emotion that Penny rarely feels and that Crystal never feels. She had wanted to step out from behind the glass and hug her as one would hug a child who has just touched a hot frying pan and is now amazed at her own wound. In the first instance of her pity, Penny told the woman to come back the following day; in the second instance, she said, *My name is Penny, pretty as a penny.* In the third and most severe, Penny agreed to have a drink with her. What Penny had not realized in those moments of familial tenderness was that in saying those words Penny and Crystal had become the same person.

But they were not the same person. They could never be the same person. If one ever folded into the other, Penny would die. So she erases the image of the woman's eyes from her mind, disposing of it as she has many memories before this one. When she emerges from her thoughts, the light has changed slightly so that now she can see her own reflection in the window glass, her eyes flat and cold. She walks to the telephone and dials Sex World. "I won't be in tomorrow," she says. "I don't feel well," she says. "I can't work like this," she says. There is always someone else anyway—younger, firmer flesh—willing to climb into the box and await another disciple. She sits back in the window, her initial pity turned to disgust. She traces a fingertip down the cold window glass. She will spend the next day solely as Penny, reading magazines, ordering Chinese takeout, and watching the city she lives in from high above, living in her own small, carefully constructed geography. Both Penny and Crystal will be safe again.

At Sex World the next day, Mary nods at the stringy-haired clerk and walks to Penny's booth, but the booth is empty, a vacant storefront. Her heartbeat doubles and like a front, she blows back to the counter, surprising herself with her own ferocity.

"We don't have anyone here named Penny," the stingy-haired clerk insists.

Mary's fists are clenched atop the counter and have started turning white. "I'm not an idiot," she says. "I know you saw me in here the last two days in a row."

"Do you know how many people come through here on any given day?" he asks. His teeth are clogged with bits of the sandwich that sits next to him on the counter.

"Listen, she told me her name was Penny and she told me to come in today."

He gives her an especially greasy smile. "I bet she did."

"I'm not just some dirty prick regular, OK?"

"I didn't say you were."

"So where is Penny?"

36

"I told you. No Penny. We have a Crystal, a Destiny, a Fantasie, and a Starr. There is no Penny."

Mary stares at him, saying nothing for a moment. "Right. I'll be back tomorrow," she says, rapping her knuckles on the counter. "I'll see you tomorrow night."

As she walks toward the door, the betrayal wells in her eyes. Had even Penny decided she was worthless? Outside, the city dies all around her. The only colors untouched by the snow drain from the streets, and everything left is cast in grayscale. Shocks run up her legs as she pounds the concrete, and her knee burns. She cannot hear her own footsteps; she cannot hear anything except a dull, insistent ringing. *Let it go,* she tells herself. However, she cannot let go, for if she does, this time she knows she will not struggle to unmoor the hook. *I will go back tomorrow*, she tells herself.

The next day, Mary enters Sex World and glares at the stringy-haired clerk. Penny is sitting there just as Mary imagined, her blonde hair perfect, the same *Lusty Lady* T-shirt draped over her. The sight of her calms Mary, but her anger does not dissipate, not yet. "Penny," she says. Penny looks up, startled, but says nothing. Then she stands and reaches behind the chair for something. In the light, the cellulite on the backs of her thighs glows. Mary bites the side of her lip, enjoying the pain. She slides a twenty into the slot. Penny's shoulders drop and she turns around. "You weren't here yesterday," Mary says.

"Now, I'm sorry, darlin'. I was tired and I went home early."

"That's what it is?"

"Yes, darlin', that's all. Just tired and seeing as how I didn't have a way to call you, there wasn't really anything I could do. But now, I'm here. How are you, darlin'?"

"I'm fine."

"Just fine?"

"I want you to have a drink with me."

Penny sighs. "Darlin', I'm not a drinking buddy."

"We can go out for coffee then," she says, the words sticking in her throat because something has already changed between them. She can see it in Penny's eyes; they are different now, gray, flat.

"I'm your friend here." She gestures at the booth. "Isn't that good enough?"

"I want the person I talked to the day before yesterday. I want that person back."

"I'm right here."

Mary's body is riddled with latent tension; she shifts her hips, stretches her aching knee. What she wants is to mine Penny for something, for anything that will bind them. "Don't you see? Not everyone's black and blue like we are," she says.

"We? You included me pretty quickly," Penny says. "You shouldn't assume darlin'. It isn't becoming."

Mary grinds her teeth, thinking of yesterday, of the clerk and his scummy teeth. *We don't have a Penny.* She longs to puncture Penny's facade until the facade becomes lace, the sinews of it fine enough to see through.

"Don't posture. It isn't becoming," she says.

"Posturing?" Penny says. The artifice of her speech is suddenly gone.

"You aren't Starr or Destiny or Crystal. You told me your real name. You're Penny."

Penny leans into the glass. "I want you to listen to me closely. My name is Crystal. This is who Crystal is and every time you walk into this place, you're seeing Crystal. Are we square on that?"

"I don't care about Crystal. It's Penny I want."

"Damn it!" she says, slapping the glass with her palm. Mary jerks backward. The sound rings through the booth. "Are you not fucking listening to me? Leave it alone. Leave Penny out of this."

"Penny would want to know why I did it. Penny would be asking me right now."

Before Penny can respond, the doors fly open and light floods the booth. The stringy-haired clerk rips the phone out of Mary's hands. "She bothering you, Crystal?" he says.

Mary freezes, looking from the clerk to Penny and back again.

"Her time's up."

"You need to put in more money or leave," the stringy-haired clerk says. "Those are the rules."

"Well, darlin'," Penny says, "what's it going to be?"

Penny and the stringy-haired clerk stare at her, her indecision mounting under their gaze. Aside from their staring at her, this moment is no different from the others: turning off her alarm instead of going to school, stepping off the pail, decisions which had alienated her, decisions, which in retrospect had been wrong. She smiles at the clerk, then looks into Penny's eyes and slides another twenty into the bill slot.

"Thata girl," the stringy-haired clerk says. "Crystal, let me know if you need anything," he adds.

"Sure," she says, slamming down the receiver.

He lingers for a moment before walking out, the doors swinging shut behind him, the booth returning to its private glow. Mary holds onto the phone for another moment, waiting. Penny does not pick it up again. Finally, Mary places it back on the hook and sits down. The glass, which had once seemed permeable, has lost its permeability, and although she now knows it will stay this way, she thinks it better to watch someone else than to keep looking at herself. So, for a while she simply watches Penny, their eyes in a wintery deadlock. Then a song playing in the store ends, and as a new one begins, Penny stands up on the chair as though it is an act of defiance and begins swaying her hips. She peels off her T-shirt. Then, she turns away from Mary, carefully shimmying out of her tight black mini-skirt. As she dances, Mary repeats her new name. *Crystal,* she says, *Crystal,* the syllables hard, unpalatable. But when Penny finally turns around, her large breasts bared, breasts clinging to the last of their youth, the name slides into place.

THE GARBAGE COLLECTOR

Across Minneapolis, murders of crows were roosting. They floated through the purple darkness on winter wind like hundreds of small trash liners and then landed and littered the trees. When Ray passed beneath them while returning from the daily routine he had established since retiring a few months ago—a trip downtown for coffee—he wasn't sure if what he heard was the rhythmic stretch and flap of their wings or the splattering of their yellow-white shit on the branches, the cars, the sidewalks. If the shit-covered blocks were not bad enough, winter had dallied and flirted with the city, now blowing in from the North, now blowing in from the South, so that everything was in a stasis of slip. Ray did not see the patch of ice on which he slipped, nor did he see the stain his spilled cup of coffee made on the snow. One moment he was standing; the next he was having a lucid dream.

In his dream, he was on a city bus. The bus was warm and his glasses were just starting to defog. A child pointed and laughed at him until her mother slapped her hand away.

"It's OK," Ray said, reaching out and tousling her hair. They laughed, everyone, the whole bus, a long laugh as if they were stars in a somnambulant sitcom. Then, before he knew it, the bus came to his stop. As he stood and walked to the front with his hands outstretched at his sides, the other passengers began handing him things—candy wrappers, used Kleenexes, ripped mittens, half-eaten sandwiches—and his hands were large enough to hold it all. The passengers looked up at him, their gratefulness akin to awe. Then, in the driver's seat, he recognized his daughter. She turned and waved at him and dropped orange peels in his hand. He was happy, he knew he was happy, and his happiness put itself on his lips as his daughter opened the door to the bus, and then …

"Sir—sir, are you OK?"

He turned his head to see an older woman standing next to him.

"I was just coming out and I saw you lying down here. And I thought to myself, I had better go see if he's OK. He doesn't look like someone I'd expect to see lying on the sidewalk like that, no way. Are you OK?"

It took him a minute to find speech. "I think so."

"Do you need a doctor?"

"I don't think so," he said, although he could not be sure.

"Do you know where you are?"

"Nicollet and Thirty-Sixth."

She nodded. "And who's the president?"

41

"Barack Obama."

"Yes, God bless him. And what year is it?"

"2012."

"What's your name?"

"Ray."

"Sounds like you're right as rain, Ray. Why don't you come in and sit down for a minute. I've got coffee on. I was just coming out to run to the store quick."

"That's all right. You don't have to—"

"Nonsense. You need to warm up for the rest of your walk."

"OK," he said, reasoning that maybe sitting down for a few minutes to make sure no real damage had been done would be best.

He stood and collected himself, straightening his hat, jacket, and slacks, which now had coffee splatters on the legs. Then he remembered the birds. He turned his head and looked at the back of his pants, which were spotted with shit. He touched the back of his head, his fingertips pulling the wet paste out of his hair. He looked around until he found the birds in the trees a few blocks away, where they hung like ornaments, lifeless until one or two suddenly erupted into motion, circled, and then landed on a different branch. Their intermittent cries sailed into Ray's ears.

"God damn it. God damn birds," he muttered.

"What's that?"

"The birds."

The woman laughed, which made him want to go into her house even less. He did not feel right though—he was sweating and his back and head shared the same dull ache. Feeling that way made him nervous, and he quickly reasoned that resting and drinking some water would help.

After less than a half block, the woman turned off the sidewalk and toward an old house half-hidden by ratty pine trees. He followed her into the kitchen and sat down at the table while she busied herself making coffee. She was short and her face had all the deep valleys of those who had earned their age by smoking. Her long black and gray hair, slightly stringy, was parted so that a red barrette held back one side. She wore all red: her red slacks matched a red sweater. Underneath the sweater was a turtleneck, washed one too many times so that it did not match the vibrancy of her other clothes. Ray knew her type—she was one of those old women who had become obsessed with one color. He saw them out shopping—red ladies, blue ladies, purple ladies, and he remembered them from when he was still working, the homogeneity of their trash. As he surveyed the kitchen, red accents popped out as though his eyes were being tested at the doctor's office—red paper napkins, red plastic flowers, red curtains. Yes, she was one of them. Unfortunately, he thought, she was probably the same age as he was.

"Dangerous out there in the winter. Lots of broken bones," she said. "The little girl right across the street fell on her way to the bus stop and broke her arm last week. Yes sir, that's a shame, all right."

Ray nodded. He had never liked this type of small talk. Even now, shit-speckled and dazed, he felt as though a large palm were squeezing his stomach.

"I used to work in a hospital, you know. That's how I knew to ask you those questions. When someone would come in after a fall, the nurses would ask them those things. If they couldn't answer, you knew it wasn't good. It *was not* good." She paused, sipping her coffee. "Sally's the name. So, Ray, what do you do?"

Ray stared into his cup. That question always put him off. He had been retired only three months, but already everyone seemed to treat him differently, and he hated it. "I was a garbage man. Thirty-five years," he said, giving her his standard answer. Saying his occupation in the past tense instead of saying "I am retired" seemed to change the emphasis of the statement. He thought that just maybe it stopped people from asking him the follow-up question he detested.

"So what are you doing now?" Sally asked.

Ray took a deep breath. Today he did not have the patience to invent a litany of activities with which he was filling his time. "A little of this. A little of that. I plan to visit my daughter some time. She's in Florida." It was true: one of these winters he *did* plan to visit his daughter in Florida. Even as he said it, he thought how silly it sounded as a retirement plan. Trips were something that non-retired people took. One trip was not a retirement plan. He quickly followed her question with a question so there was no room for her to pry. "What do you do?"

"Oh, I'm retired, too." She turned her face up toward him. "It's funny, you know? Doesn't it seem like some people never fully get how to be retired? No sir, they don't. It's like they can't figure out what to do. Not me. Not me at all." Just then, a cat came out from under the table and rubbed itself against her legs. She leaned down and stroked its back. "Isn't that right, Mr. Pickles? We've been having a great time since I retired. Can you say hi to our guest, Mr. Pickles?"

While Sally continued a lengthy conversation with the cat, Ray imagined how life was before retirement. What he remembered was standing on his back porch in the half-darkness of early mornings, smoking a cigarette and drinking a cup of coffee. Downtown Minneapolis looked like a hand reaching up into the sky. The sky was a cloth, now black, now purple, now orange and just before it exploded into sun and blue, he would be on the road in his truck, watching the world wake up, gathering all that had been left behind. There was comfort in that, a sort of heroism, the reliable heroism that people only recognized in its absence. Now that he no longer had a duty, a task, he realized just how bored he was.

He had himself.

He had a daughter halfway across the country.

He had pictures of her first house, the one he hadn't seen yet.

"Ray …?"

He snapped out of his thoughts, trying to ease the tension in his head by rolling his neck and shoulders.

"You sure you don't want me to call someone to pick you up? You were staring off a little."

"No—it's nothing, a little sore is all. Listen, I really appreciate this. The coffee and everything, but I better go home." He did not know whether he actually felt better, but he was going to take his chances and leave.

"I'm sure you have places to go and people to see."

Ray imagined his empty house, the answering machine whose light would not be blinking. "Yes, I sure do," he said. "Thanks again." He stood up from the table and walked to the door.

"No problem. Be careful walking," Sally said as she led him out.

Outside, the crows were nowhere to be seen, which made him feel better. He walked carefully down the block a bit before turning and looking back toward Sally's house. She was there in the doorframe, the red doorframe, watching him walk away. For a second he felt compelled to wave, but he did not want to wave. He did not want to be friendly with people who had succumbed to the lure of one color and the companionship of cats.

As he continued walking, half-snow-covered pieces of litter distracted him. Why wouldn't people just put their trash in garbage cans? There was *a whole industry* based on collecting other people's trash. He stopped to pick up a few items in the middle of the sidewalk: an empty Milwaukee's Best Light can; a crumpled McDonald's bag; a damp, crushed pack of Marlboros. As he dumped them, he could not help but look down into the can. Its contents were disappointingly congruent with what he had just tossed. These standard issue city garbage cans were dull. After having been a garbage man for so long, what interested him was the trash associated with specific houses, specific people. He had operated a rear loader, and when the sweeper blade came down, he watched the bags split open—ribbons of lives showing through the plastic. Here an uneaten head of lettuce, here a discarded shoe, here pieces of mail, here an old dress. Everything in those bags once had lives, lives that had reached their end in the compactor. He had stood and watched reverently as they succumbed to their fate. Someone had to give them dignity.

When he finally got home, he wanted nothing more than to settle in front of the television and watch a ballet. A few years before retirement, he had taken to watching ballets although he had never cared for dancing and

44

had never been persuaded—except at a few weddings—to set foot on a dance floor. Then one night as he sat home alone, his twenty-year marriage breaking around him, he stumbled onto a performance of the Miami Ballet on Twin Cities Public Television. He did not know the name of the ballet he was watching, nor did he particularly care what it was or what music was playing. He remembered hitting the mute button on the television. Then he remembered how the light and movements drew him in until he could not extricate himself. His ex-wife, had she caught him watching, would have thought he was watching for the bodies, the young bodies whose thighs, stomachs, and breasts had not yet been ravaged by cellulite or sun damage. But that wasn't it. They were not people to him. To him the dancers were parts of moving stories, gears that spun infallibly through their time on the stage. All he knew was that when everything was falling apart, the stories— filled with resplendent tragedies and fabled endings—gave him hope. He needed that; he needed hope.

He sat in his recliner to watch one of his tapes, which in his effort to hide his interest from his ex-wife's scrutiny, he had not labeled. As soon as *Swan Lake* started though, he grew anxious. This version was not the one he wanted; this was the version where the curtain fell on the male lead standing on stage alone. The ending was not right. He wished he had never kept it. He did not like thinking of the man like that, all that solitary, empty time in front of him. People like that were similar to the homeless: a primal fear associated with homelessness was time, having so much time. Humans were like hamsters or other rodents. They needed wheels. However, eventually the body—in all the humor of the human condition—began to wear so that it could no longer spin its wheel. That was when Ray's young coworkers had started lifting things for him. "I'll get it, Ray," they said, even though Ray had not asked. "This is a big one," they said. Soon it became clear to him that he had reached and exceeded his prime. It had been time to retire. Even thinking about it now got him angry.

As he tried to settle into another tape, he could not stop thinking of Sally. Like a piece of sand in his eye or a rock in his shoe, the woman was an irritant. Right now, she was probably home alone watching television too, but with that damn cat curled up on the couch beside her. His legs twitched, and he shifted in his seat. Finally, he just stopped the tape and took a deep breath. He knew what he needed: he needed to call his daughter. A visit to Florida was overdue. Plus, he had told Sally his plan, and that statement loomed over him like a contract. He had never been a talker, and he certainly could not let this plan fall to talk when he had divulged it to a woman like her.

He got up and dialed Lisa.

"Hello?" a man's voice on the line said.

"This is Lisa's dad. She there?"

"Oh, hey Ray."

"I know you?"

"Sorry. I'm Lisa's boyfriend," he said, remaining silent when most would have revealed a name.

"You have a name?"

"Rory."

"Rory, can I talk to my daughter, please?"

"Sure," he said, yelling Lisa's name with the phone not far enough from his mouth for the comfort of Ray's ear.

After a minute, Ray heard the jumble of the phone being handed over with some giggling and then Lisa's voice coming through.

"Hello?"

"Letting him answer your phone already?"

"Already?"

"First I've heard of him."

"It's been a couple months."

"How are you?" he said, steering her away from that subject.

"I'm good. Busy with teaching." Lisa was a yoga instructor. She ate things from plants Ray had never heard of and read books about the Tao and Buddhism. She wore long skirts and sandals and Ray shuddered when he thought of the itinerant, dreadlocked men who had been in and out of her bedroom over the years.

"Say, I was thinking I could come down."

"Wow."

"Wow what?"

"Just unexpected, that's all. You didn't come when I bought the house and threw the big party that half the family came to—including your brother."

"I had my reasons."

"Right."

"Your mom was bringing *him*, OK?"

"You know Buddhist monks spend days making sand mandalas only to destroy them and throw the sand into the river. It's called letting go."

"Christ Almighty. Here we go."

"Are you going to act like an asshole if you come?"

"I'm not trying to act like an asshole, OK? Sorry. When can I come? I want to see you."

"End of the month? How long are you staying?"

"That works. How long do you want me?"

"However long you want. Hang on a sec …."

He could hear Rory's voice in the background.

"Shit, dad, I have to go. Rory and I are late for our vegan cooking class. Call me when you get dates."

And then she was gone.

46

But he had the promise of his daughter and the sun.

He had the ballet.

He had the idea that maybe he could take his daughter to the ballet.

Ray was still restless when he hung up the phone. He supposed he should start looking up fares, but instead he opened a beer and wondered what it would be like visiting her. He wondered if Rory, who he had imagined to be some slack-jawed surfer, would try to befriend him, addressing him informally, and hiding little about the relationship he had with Lisa. When he was young, people did not talk as openly as they did now, and they seemed stronger. They regarded life more ambivalently. Things were what they were. That had been OK with him until now, for now he fully realized that he was not merely on vacation. Vacation ended; retirement did not. Ambivalence now would surely kill him.

The next day as the crows circled, he bought his ticket to Florida.

When his plane landed in Orlando a few weeks later, he first noticed the light. It was softer than the winter light he had come from—it did not brutalize his eyes. He peeled off his jacket and raised his arms, letting the air wrap around them and flow into his short shirtsleeves. One of the Midwest's greatest tricks was that every winter you forgot what the air felt like on your skin. Then suddenly as though a small gift were being bestowed upon you, the first warm day broke open and you pulled off your sweater or coat or sweatshirt and stretched your arms out into it. That one moment of touch was worth enduring the winter, as it were, all six months of frigidness. This was the moment he had as he waited for his daughter to arrive.

When she pulled into the pickup lane, she was alone, thankfully. He was relieved that Rory or another minor character in her life would not immediately affront him. He was also relieved because it would be easier to ask her to see the ballet with him if she were alone. He did not want Rory to know about the ballet. He did not want to share the ballet with anyone but Lisa.

"Daddy!" she said, opening her arms and hugging him with a ferocity he did not expect.

"Hi, baby," he said, hugging her and taking in her scent, still familiar though they had not lived together for ten years.

She popped the trunk of her beat-up Civic, the rear bumper donning an Equality sticker, and he threw his bag in the trunk.

"I was thinking about something," he said.

"What's that?"

"I was thinking we could see the ballet."

She started laughing.

"Forget it," he snapped.

"I'm sorry," she said, "the ballet?"

47

"Yes, the goddamn ballet. I want to go to the ballet."

"The ballet."

"Does it have to be such a big thing? You and your mother both. Jesus." But even as he said it, he knew those women had been his whole world. He wished it had been easier to spend more time with his daughter after the divorce, but it had been hard: with every salty sentiment and subsequent girlish giggle, Lisa reminded him of her mother. He would never admit that sometimes he had not called her for that reason, but the worst of it was over now, and he was relieved.

"Do you have one in mind that you want to go to?" she asked even though he thought he could hear laughter in the spectrum of her voice.

"No, not really," he said. "I just want to see one in person."

"I get it, dad. I just didn't know you were a fan," she said, and then unlike his ex-wife would have, she accepted it and drove them through the low and small neighborhoods, neighborhoods full of sprawling trees covered in Spanish moss. Finally, they pulled up to her house.

Her small living room was decorated with modern, angular furniture, Asian paintings, and small plants. He fumbled awkwardly with his shoes, surveying his surroundings and looking for a place to make his own. As though she sensed it, "Extra bedroom's over there," Lisa said. There were times he knew unequivocally that she was his daughter.

"I'm going to lay down. Wake me up if I sleep too long."

"I will," she said, squeezing his hand.

He organized himself in the extra bedroom, which was accented with deep orange pillows and curtains, and though the room itself was relaxing, he couldn't sleep. His thoughts were birds that flew and landed and flew and landed, crying shrilly. After a while, he simply gave up, and when he came back out, his daughter was eating a carton of yogurt and watching a cooking program on TV.

"Put on your going-out clothes, Dad," she said. "I got us tickets."

"Yeah? What's the ballet?"

"Orlando Ballet Theater. It's called *Swans: Black and White*. Is that OK?"

"Yeah, that's—that's more than OK," he said. He felt his face redden, and he looked down to hide it.

"I bet you wish you had come sooner now, huh?" she said, poking his shoulder.

He mussed her hair, ruining the carefully constructed part—something he used to do when she was a teenager.

"Dad!" she whined. "Go get dressed!"

As he turned away from her, his stomach rose and dropped in excitement and he couldn't help but laugh, which he did quietly and to himself.

Over dinner, she pushed rice and vegetables around her plate with chopsticks as her cheeks flushed and she talked about her job and her house and all the plans she had for the next year. He felt better being near her—all that youth and enthusiasm. Her presence bolstered him so that he felt full and stronger than he had when he left Minneapolis. He did wish he had come sooner. He wished he had been stronger after the divorce and could have ignored his ex-wife and her new lover, some middle-management pencil-pusher she met at work. But as Lisa continued talking, he knew there was no reason to think about that now.

By the time they got to the theater, darkness had fallen. The temperature had dropped. While they waited in line, his daughter took his arm and for just a moment rested her head on his shoulder as she had done when she was little.

"Where's what's his name?" Ray asked.

"Rory's working. You'll see him tomorrow."

"Lucky me."

"Christ," she said, and they both started laughing. They had drunk a bottle of wine and he felt loose and good, and they did not need to talk much now.

As they walked in the theater, Ray's pulse quickened. The theater itself was grander than he had imagined, and Lisa had gotten them good seats, right in the center.

"How much were these?" he asked after they sat down.

"Never mind," she said, patting his hand.

"Just because I'm retired doesn't mean I can't—"

"Why don't you just say thanks, Dad?" She was smiling her Lisa smile, the mischievous one she had, and when he looked at her face, he could never tell how old she was. He saw all of her life at once.

"Thanks," he said, "thanks, baby."

"Now wasn't that easier than fighting about it?"

"I'll never admit it."

"I know," she said, and they both laughed again.

Soon the lights went down and then the curtain raised and the dancers appeared on stage, thin, muscular, and stoic. The ballerinas' costumes glowed in the light. Their hands and jawlines, their pirouettes, arabesques and grand jetés were perfect. Tchaikovsky rang out from the orchestra pit, wrapped itself around him, and soon he was no longer separate from the performance or the performers. He was a part of it, of them, as it and they were a part of him. The music moved his chest and his body soared with the dancers' movements. Before he knew it, tears had collected in his eyes, and he had the urge to reach out and hold his daughter's hand. He struggled to contain his tears, but at least a couple made their way down his face, which he furtively wiped away with the back of his hand. It was so much beauty for one day. This was a gift he had received, a piece of light he would hold onto until the day he died.

After a week that passed easily despite Rory's hippy ramblings, Ray was back in Minneapolis, where crows and wet snow greeted him. Too soon, the glow of the trip cooled, and the feeling that he had gotten something new, that something had changed, left him.

One morning he woke early to more heavy snow. He lay in half-darkness and loneliness, missing his daughter and the warmth of Florida. To occupy himself, he began imagining the city around him. The red woman would be making a pot of bitter coffee and feeding her cat, uninterested in the garbage trucks that pulled into the alleys of Minneapolis. The crows would dive, swoop, and hop in the streets eating the flesh of dead squirrels and rabbits. The garbage collectors, full of coffee and smelling of their first cigarettes, would jump down off trucks, their boots making prints in the snow. They would notice the difference in weight as they lifted the snow-covered lids of the cans. Then, they would empty them into the compactor where the bags containing the remnants of lives would be gutted. The garbage collectors would watch this, some with indifference; some, like Ray, with reverence.

He rolled on his side and then on his back, and then on his side and on his back. Finally, he could not stand to lie there anymore. He could think of only one thing to do to make himself feel better, so he got up, put on his boots, coat, scarf, and hat, and walked through his back door, across the yard, and into the alley. Starting at one end of the alley and working his way east toward where the sun would rise, he began clearing the snow off the tops of the garbage cans, positioning them all so their mouths faced the alley. His heartbeat and breath increased; a sweat collected on his brow. The cold no longer bothered him, nor did his thoughts. A blessed blankness settled on him as he worked, and before long, he had cleaned off three alleys' worth of cans. Finally, at the end of the next alley, he bowed deeply, retrieving the small skeleton of some discarded item from beneath the snow, which he put in his pocket before turning to walk home.

THE LEAVING KIND

It was Monday morning, and the unpolluted day was before Janet. This was her favorite time, her breath unspent because no one had spoken to her and she had spoken to no one, so a cross word or a miscommunication was not even possible. She stared out the window of her yellow kitchen, watching a small mound of powdered snow blow off the porch railing on the late January wind. As she drank hot tea and ate an apple, she heard Bradley, her son, start down the stairs.

"Morning, Mom," he said.

"Morning, love. Oatmeal's on the stove. No raisins."

"OK," he said, walking heavily across the faded linoleum toward the stove. He filled a bowl and took it into the living room. A minute later, Janet heard the television switch on and the couch squeak. Now that he was nearly eighteen, taller than she was, he no longer sat at the table with her for breakfast. She had not fought him on this; rather, she had watched him make the change as a spectator would. It was strange, she thought, for mothers with sons. Sons became something else altogether: men. Bradley had grown muscled and strong—stronger than she was—a fact that lingered with her.

She cleared away her dishes and dressed for her job as a bus driver with Metro Transit. When she was ready, she called for Bradley so she could drop him off at school on her way to work. South Minneapolis was in the grip of winter, just like the whole Midwest. Breath and exhaust and steam, signs of life, were visible in clouds that dissipated as quickly as they were born. Today was cold enough that her passengers would look especially grateful when she opened the door of the bus, a blanket on her lap to protect herself from each burst of cold air that rushed in.

"Just another beautiful day," she said, as she and Bradley began driving down Cedar Avenue.

He grunted.

"Do you have anything going on after school tonight?"

"No."

"See you at dinner then, right?"

"Yeah. Jeremy's going to give me a ride home. Just no stuffed peppers tonight, please?"

"No stuffed peppers. Jeremy can stay if he wants."

She pulled up in front of his school—away from the parking lot where all the kids whose parents or who themselves could afford cars parked. Though Bradley had been saving money, he had not yet found a car he could afford. His having a car would mean another removal between them, and

Janet was happy he had not found one. She soothed his frustration by allowing him to use her Ford on Friday and Saturday nights, nights on which she asked few questions about what he did, creating the illusion she didn't worry about him every time he left the house. Though she longed to cling to him, she did not want him to see that in her, a lesson she had learned about people long ago. Before he opened the door to get out of her Ford, she put a hand on the back of his neck, feeling the small, fine hairs at its base. They smiled at each other, and then he was gone.

She parked her car in the lot at the garage and her day began. In the years she had spent as a bus driver, she concluded that buses never really went anywhere; rather, they just orbited. On the 22 route, she drove down North Lyndale where the yards alternated between twisted beds of weeds and neatly edged squares of grass; through the Camden neighborhood, past its liquor and convenience stores, its Laundromats and barbershops; and then on to Shingle Creek Parkway where the houses were bigger, spaced farther apart, and fewer people waited at the stops. She had learned the true geography of the city from watching the changing faces that stepped on the bus, each representative of its own world along the route. She ferried her passengers safely to their stops, opening her door and then closing it behind them. When they left, she wondered after them, even though it was a relationship she knew well: she maintained a constant loop so that passengers could ride with her until their stops came, at which point they stepped off, often without acknowledging her. There were places in her route—sometimes when she left downtown—that she had no passengers at all. During those times, the bus sounded and felt different, like an empty tin can bumbling along an invisible track, and it made her feel as if the whole city were empty, too.

That night, as she waited for Bradley to come home, she poured herself two fingers of Jameson over ice. She sat near the living room window watching the empty trees, thinking about how she would soon be forty. She was unmarried and had never been to college. There was still time, though, she thought, to start a real career or a relationship, although she would not know how to begin either. She had made certain sacrifices, as single mothers do, but she did not allow herself to think of them often. She did not pity herself; she thought of herself as person who had made sensible choices given her circumstances. However, as Bradley grew up, the fact that she had no real career and would be alone in the house when he moved out weighed on her, for if she was not a wife or a mother with a child at home, who would she be? A lonely bus driver with a rotating cast of static characters.

Janet swallowed the rest of her whiskey just as Bradley's friend, Jeremy, who drove a dilapidated Chevy, pulled into the driveway. They were laughing, and she imagined that Bradley would smell a little like cigarettes when he walked into the house, though she had not yet figured out which one of them smoked or if it was both of them. She knew Bradley already had a life

52

the radio. The night slipped forth into darkness, and like wet snow, waiting fell upon her.

She resumed her seat in the window and stared at a pickup truck with "J and J Construction" emblazoned on the side parked beneath the streetlight. The driver got out and kicked at the hardened snow that had accumulated above one of the tires. The truck and the man reminded her of Bradley's father, and she began thinking of him as she sometimes still did. Though when she imagined him now, she did not picture him from memories of their time together; rather, she imagined him in a kitchen in some other city, waiting with a cup in hand for coffee to percolate, or lathering his face with shaving cream, then making one clean pass at his cheek with a razor. She liked to imagine him turning on the shower, flushing the toilet, engrossed in all the mundane activities of daily life.

Bradley's father, Carl, was a construction worker. Janet met him at a party in a May, many Mays ago. By June they had become lovers and by August, she was pregnant. He stayed with her through that winter, hunkered down in a studio apartment, bassinet in the corner. They ate beef stew, watched television programs, and lay on the couch as snow fell down on La Salle Avenue. Bradley was born late the following spring. By June, as she nursed the baby, she noticed more and more that Carl's eyes wandered out the window off toward Loring Park. Still, she clung desperately to him—her happiness. Soon it was July and she knew that before August, he would be gone, for he was the leaving kind: a season onto himself. Maybe she had known this about him all along, but when she was young, she had moved with her heart, an animal of desire, of passion, too young to recognize that animals who move as such are the ones first ensnared. Carl had taught her one of the quintessential differences between herself and others: she was not the leaving kind, but she would forever be attracted to those who were.

During Bradley's early years, Carl kept in loose contact with them, but the summer after Bradley's first-grade year, all contact stopped. After, Janet explained to Bradley what she had learned about his father, that he was the leaving kind. She thought Bradley was too young to understand, but he had never asked many questions afterwards, so perhaps he had understood. Janet thought it was a lesson best learned early. Since learning it herself, she had only taken a lover or two to satisfy her flesh, never allowing a relationship beyond that communion. She had an identity: she called herself mother, and so she did not need men or the danger they posed any longer.

It was late when Bradley returned in his new car, and Janet was angry that he had not come home immediately as she had told him to, but he had been so happy and she did not want to ruin it, not today. When he came in the door smiling and asked her to, she walked out in her bathrobe to inspect the car.

"I should have worn a jacket," she said, crossing her arms around herself.

He opened their garage door so some light shone out onto the car. "You have to see how clean the engine is," he said, fumbling to reach the lever under the hood. When the hood was open, he retrieved a flashlight from the garage. "Here, take a look," he said, panning the extra light around the engine. "Great, isn't it?"

"Yeah. It's nice, love, very clean."

"Come and sit down," he said, opening the passenger door for her.

She climbed in and he began demonstrating all the features of his decrepit little gem.

"I'm going to start it up." He turned over the ignition and then stepped lightly on the accelerator.

"Pretty quiet for an old beater," he smiled.

Janet was looking at the ceiling; the soft fabric had begun to sag, and the door to the glove box sat like a crooked tooth.

"Yes, it is," she said. "Excited, huh?"

He smiled and then looked down at his shoes as though he had been caught. "Now you won't have to drive me to school anymore."

"No, I guess I won't."

"Or pick me up."

"You're right," she said softly.

They listened to the engine for another minute, and then she opened her door.

"I'm going to go to bed. Come in soon. It's already getting late."

"I will."

The next morning he was awake before she was.

"Thinking about your new toy already?" she asked.

He shrugged and poured himself a bowl of cereal. They moved around each other in the kitchen silently and then he left and went into the living room, turning on the television. Janet drank her tea and got ready for work. She had nearly forgotten that today she would drive there by herself.

They left the house together, and before he pulled away, she leaned into the window of his car. "Be careful. Come home right after school. No detours today, OK?"

"Sure, Mom," he said, fiddling with the radio.

"And don't mess with that while you're driving. My sister put a car in the ditch that way."

"OK, OK," he said.

With that, he pulled away and Janet watched him. Part of her wanted to start her car as quickly as possible and tail him all the way to school, but she knew that she could not do that. She stood helpless as his car disappeared from sight, thinking about how Bradley was made of half his father.

56

After work that night, she let the radio fill the empty house while she prepared dinner. By the time dinner was ready, Bradley had not come home. She began eating without him and still he did not come home. When she had finished her meal and the rest of the pasta was cooling on the stove, still he did not come home. Her son was somewhere; there was no such thing as nowhere, so she fell to imagining somewhere: the city with all its neighborhoods, and at the center, downtown, its streets alternating between hope and hopelessness, its crown jewel the statue of Mary Tyler Moore with her hand perpetually reaching for a hat she would never catch. Yes, she could imagine the city itself swallowing her son whole. There was so much about it he did not yet know. She contemplated calling Jeremy's mother to see if she knew anything about where Bradley might be. Then she thought about getting in her Ford and driving around to see if his car was parked outside any of his friends' houses. However, she would not allow herself to any of these things; they were too public, the gestures too grandiose.

She began pacing around the house, his blatant disobedience gnawing at her, a predator pulling the sinews of its prey. She walked past his room three times before finally walking in and turning on the light. His room, as always, was neat, all the clothes folded and put away. Even the top of his desk was free of stray papers. A calendar hanging above it counted down to his eighteenth birthday; there were fewer than sixty days left. The carpet was clean because he always took his shoes off at the front door. The only thing marring the room was a stray white sock, peaking from beneath the bed. She picked it up and held it to her nose. It was soft and smelled like the detergent they always kept in the house. She set it on top of his bed and sat down on the blue plaid comforter. From the time Bradley was a child, he had always liked his things neat. He required few reprimands, assuming responsibility for himself. Tending him was always how she thought of being his mother. He only ever required tending. She leaned forward and opened his blinds. His window looked out and into the neighbor's house. Through the window she could see Brenda rocking a tiny baby in a pink onesie to sleep. She remembered Brenda having said something about pregnancy in the summer, but in the cold of late fall and winter, neighbors did not talk so much, and she had forgotten that a new baby would be living next door. The sight of them together made her remember what it was like to have a baby, to have a warm body that needed you, that needed more than just tending.

She glanced back at Bradley's desk—a small wooden thing that had been painted and repainted. Currently it had blue drawers. She swallowed and did not allow herself to think. With hands of impulse, she walked to the desk and began pulling out the drawers. Like everything else in the room, they were orderly. At first, she moved through them gently, guiltily, but then she clawed through them, a thief with limited time. Her heart begged her to search, to search for clues as to who she lived with now. Soon she had

57

emptied the drawers out onto the floor. She found a girl's phone number on a scrap of paper that had a cherry printed on the corner. There was a lighter. She flicked it, letting it burn until the heat reached her thumb. A familiar desperation urged her dig deeper. She did not replace the dresser drawers or their contents. Instead, she moved onto the closet, sure she would find something there, something definitive. She pulled his button-downs from the bar they hung on and lay them on the bed. She inspected the corners of the closet, finding a shoebox. She brought it out in the light and held it for a moment. Sitting Indian-style on the floor, she pulled back the lid. The box was filled with baseball cards—collectibles he had abandoned long ago. Underneath them were a few cards from his father. Janet opened one and rubbed her fingers across Carl's signature. She could still feel the indentations borne of his hand.

There with the box in her lap, she began to cry, her stomach contracting, forcing her frustration to surface. After a few minutes, she wiped the tears from her eyes with the sleeve of her pink bathrobe and discarded the box. I have to be here somewhere, too, she thought. With renewed determination, she surveyed the room, turning around and around until her gaze settled on his dresser. Recklessly, she ripped the drawers from their frames, and then the clothes from the drawers. She thrust her hands in the pockets of his jeans, extracting and examining each scrap of paper, each ball of lint. She began regarding herself in the context of each item. No, she had not bought him the blue hooded sweatshirt, or the now faded Twins T-shirt, and once in her hands each article seemed foreign. What about the CDs? She began pulling them one by one from the small holder in the corner of the room. She imagined the hours and hours of sounds he listened to that she had never heard. I am nowhere to be found, she thought, nowhere at all. She stood up with the room unraveled before her, each item a word dislodged from the story of her son, and she wondered if in this house there had ever been just one story, or if there had always been two stories, stories whose movements were not mutually exclusive.

Then Bradley was in front of her, and she turned her head toward him, her mouth open.

"What the hell are you doing? You tore my whole room apart!"

"Where have you been?"

"Out."

"Answer me straight."

"I was out with Jeremy and Mike."

"Out where?"

"We just got some burgers."

"You just don't come and go like you please in this house," her voice sunk. "You do not just come and go like you please."

"It was just some burgers. I wasn't doing anything and you're acting crazy!" he said, nearly yelling.

"I don't care. I don't care how it looks."

"Why are you doing this?"

"I'm looking," she said.

"For what? What the hell are you looking for?" He stared at her blankly.

She did not know how to explain what it was she had been searching for, and so she did not try. "I own all this, you know," she said, her hands on her hips. "I own everything here. It's all mine. Everything. And you still are, too."

He set his jaw as he had the other day. "Not the car."

"I can take that from you."

"The hell you can! It's mine. I paid for it and you can't do anything about it."

"Don't talk back and don't curse at me."

"I could just get in it and drive away," he said.

"Stop it."

"It would be easy."

"Bradley—"

"I still have some money."

"Stop saying it."

"Plenty of money to get me somewhere."

"Stop thinking it."

"I'll go eventually, you know. And you won't be able to do anything about it. Nothing." He turned away, tripping over a discarded drawer. "Goddamn it!" he yelled. He kicked the drawer and the cheap wooden joints exploded, splintered fireworks.

Janet started with the explosion, and watched the pieces fall. She heard his car turn over. This is how it starts, she thought, as she heard the car pull away. Seated amongst the remnants of her son, she imagined him driving down North Lyndale, Seventh Street, Marquette, streets she had driven down so often in an empty bus. Just like one of those empty buses, the house grew overly bright, the silence tinny, and it seemed that once she stepped out of Bradley's room, she would be somewhere very far away. It was not true that buses didn't go anywhere. They let people leave worlds behind. But she was the one perpetually waiting to see if those who had left would need a ride home.

CHEMISTRY

On a Thursday night, Walter parked down the block from Russell's house—the house that was now also Maureen's—turned off his headlights, and let the motor of his old Chevy idle. Maureen had been gone for two months, and in those two months, Minneapolis had fallen into the icy palms of winter. For Walter, winter made this whole thing worse, the cold, the gray, the often-invisible slippery patches on sidewalks and streets. He pulled a can of beer out of the glove compartment, opened it, and began sipping it. The windshield wipers flapped on delay, pushing off the heavy wet snow that accumulated faster by the minute. When the windows started to fog, he turned on the defroster and suffered through its heat so he could still see the house. Russell's shutters were freshly painted; the driveway and sidewalk in front of his house were both shoveled—and recently—so that only a small amount of snow remained. He was one of those people, thought Walter, who probably shoveled every couple of hours instead of waiting until the snow stopped. The window boxes outside the house were empty—unlike Walter's, which were still populated by summer's dead marigolds—and a porch light shone bright and true. The only thing imperfect about the house was that it stood close enough to the Northeast rail yard that trains would pollute the air with their scheduled wailing, a fact in which Walter took solace.

A light was on in the front room, which, having been there for a faculty Christmas party, Walter remembered was the living room. Although the curtains were drawn, they were sheer, and their sheerness merely thinly veiled the happenings inside. He could see Russell and Maureen's figures behind the large window. One sat down, and then the other stood. Seeing only their outlines eroticized the scene: he felt like he was at a peepshow, the outline of a woman's body piquing his curiosity.

Maureen approached the window. She pulled back the curtain and cupped her hands around her face so she could see from the light into the darkness. Walter slunk down in his seat, watching her out of the corner of his eye. She was wearing a red sweater—one he bought her the last Christmas they were together, when he could never even imagined her leaving—and he could still picture how the fabric felt stretched across her breasts. Blood started rushing to his groin, but this quickly stopped as he evaluated the utter ridiculousness of his current position: sitting outside his almost ex-wife's new house like some lonely old Peeping Tom. "Maureen," he said, thinking that somehow, she would hear him, but then a train started lumbering down the tracks, its horn blasting out into the night. After another few seconds, Maureen disappeared, pulling a heavier set of curtains over the sheer set. The show ended. Walter had collected his empirical evidence. Maureen and Russell were in there together and there was not a damn thing he could do about it. He flipped his headlights on and pulled out from the curb.

Once at home, he sat in an orange-striped recliner that was worn through in some places. Fragments of its foam guts held fast to his stiff denims when he adjusted his position. He turned on the television and stared at it without watching, an exercise in fighting silence because in winter, he was contractually bound to his house, silence a caveat of that contract. When he actually watched the programs, they occasionally amused him, but it was the repetition, the plotted predictability that attracted him. Archetypes, casts of archetypes—tokens: man, woman, white, black, intelligent, foolish, and awkward. He watched the same people solve the same problems episode after episode. The fact that they still found solutions, that solutions existed, was what soothed him. *Yes*, they told him, *there is hope*. He drank a beer, which lasted through the last sitcom, and then he padded down the brown-carpeted hallway to his bedroom, whose bare walls were an experiment in bachelorism.

In bed, he resumed reading of *Tender is the Night*, a book he began reading before Maureen left. After reading a few pages, he reached the part where Dick tries to stand up on a board trailing a speedboat while balancing another man on his back, the part where Dick is unable. While Walter read about the failure, his face grew hot with Dick's shame. It was just one thing and Dick couldn't do it. He knew now that Dick's trajectory was set; there was nothing anyone could do for him. With that thought, Walter lost focus. He put the book down and closed his eyes. Soon, the past and present no longer seemed absolute, but two points easily moved between. As he had done every night, since she had left, he began thinking about Maureen, and with Maureen, of course, he thought about Russell.

Unlike Walter, Maureen had always been changing. Of course he resented the final change she made: the shift of her affections to his colleague, Russell, who taught English at Washburn High School, where Walter taught science. The funniest thing about her leaving him for Russell was that in certain ways, Walter thought he and Russell were actually similar. Both of their curriculums traversed well-known territory. Russell taught *Huck Finn*, *The Grapes of Wrath*, *The Great Gatsby*, works that had been mined to complete deconstruction, characters psychoanalyzed, plots picked apart, scenes broken into beats of dialogue and movement. Walter taught chemical processes: oxidation, combustion, hydrolysis, explaining in detail the well-documented coupling and uncoupling of elements when exposed to each other or to flame, oxygen, or electricity. Just like Russell's, Walter's discipline was one of deconstruction. Every type of matter could be pulled limb from limb, reduced to atoms, parts so small they were invisible. This was how the world made sense to him.

Since Maureen left, Walter had been trying to formulate an equation to explain the relationship shared by him and Russell and Maureen. Though he could not pinpoint when exactly it happened or why, he knew that he stopped tending to Maureen, and in the absence of his stewardship, tenderness itself became absent so that their marriage was formulaic, its rituals fleshless. Men did not need as much as women, he thought, and perhaps that is why he could live with Maureen while living his life as though she were not there at all. In the last several months, they had communicated largely by writing notes to one another that were left on the refrigerator door. The notes were filled with the type of lazy shorthand that would have made Russell cringe: *Gone out for coffee. Back soon. Dinner in fridge. Heat at 350 for 20 min. Back soon. Went to school to grade tests. Back soon. Dinner with Sally. Back soon.* In the notes, they were always telling each other they would be back soon, yet neither truly came back to the other. After their ten years together, it had become easy to blend their humanity so that neither truly saw the other any longer. But, Walter thought, Russell had been able to see Maureen.

Still thinking of the three of them, Walter put his body to sleep by letting each limb go limp, struggling against a dull ache in his right thigh—the pain remnants of an old skiing injury. He slowed his breathing until he felt he was hardly breathing at all. Soon the shadow of sleep overtook him, though the night would be defined by its alternating absence and presence.

*

He woke the next morning with a short temper and a cloudy head. He was tired after having had sour dreams, most of which involved Russell and Maureen. Walter could not stop thinking about Dick Diver and how he was sure to become a laughingstock. His recliner seemed hostile, its hospitality spent. He noticed how badly the living room needed repainting, and he noticed his black fingerprints on the light switch covers and on the corners of the walls. The whole place disgusted him, and yet he did not feel like leaving. His bad leg was still bothering him as it did periodically, and while normally his slight limp was nearly imperceptible, today it was pronounced.

He bumped into an end table, knocking over a red candle, which had not been lit since well before Maureen left. There beneath the layer of dust was a small fragment of a magnesium strip. Walter stared at it, and then pushed it around with his index finger. He used to pilfer things like this from school: magnesium strips, calcium and sodium chlorides, metal salts that he would light on fire, creating a show just for Maureen. The brilliance of the colors would light up her face as the metals burned hot, fast. As each new color flashed, she looked amazed. She laughed and smiled, and she always wanted him to burn more of them, to bring home new colors. When the show was over, she hugged him and kissed him, holding his arm and resting her head on his shoulder.

63

"I want a bumper sticker that says 'I love my scientist,'" she would say. Those were the nights on which their lovemaking had been most hungry, their bodies starving for one another. Yes, thought Walter, those were the good times, and there had been many of them. He swallowed hard and put the candle back down on the table.

He entered his classroom irascible, as though he had a sharp stone in his shoe, one that he could neither find nor remove. He answered questions in short phrases, avoiding eye contact with even his favorite students, who were quieter than normal, having sensed the danger of his mood. Walter was aware of his behavior, yet he could not stop it. He could not force eye contact; he could not force full sentences to come from his mouth. By lunch, he knew that the slightest alteration to his routine could cause a meltdown, so he drove home during his lunch break and prep hour, drank one bottle of beer, and did fifty push-ups and fifty sit-ups. Then he brushed his teeth thoroughly, popped a piece of peppermint gum in his mouth, and headed back to school.

The afternoon progressed, but he was still distracted. His leg continued to bother him, and in the middle of Advanced Chemistry, he let his students work in groups building models of Alkane molecules and walked to the window. Outside, he saw Russell running laps around the track. Russell had been lucky enough to have eighth period as prep time. Walter watched him carefully: the smooth gait he maintained, his trim frame, runners' calves. *It was me*, he thought, *it was all me*. It was more than his lack of tending to Maureen. It was his limp, the worn chair he insisted on keeping, his inability to finish a novel in less than three months. Even Russell's name was better. Russell: the smooth, repeated consonants. Walter: archaic and wearing.

He turned from the window and paced around the classroom, his thoughts building like static electricity so that he was afraid to touch anything or anyone for fear they would receive the charge of his thoughts. Anyone except—well, he wished Russell would stroll through the door.

When the final bell rang, Walter packed up his things and walked toward a side door of the school. Since Maureen left, he had started parking on the street to avoid parking in the same lot as Russell. In fact, he had altered his routine as much as possible in order to avoid Russell, even eating lunch alone in the classroom because he did not want to risk a chance encounter in the teachers' lounge. As he got closer to the door, he made out Russell's figure coming toward him: khaki pants, white long-sleeved shirt, paisley tie, neatly combed hair—of which he had more than Walter had—and freshly polished loafers. His neatness reminded Walter of Maureen and he felt himself grow hot thinking about his plaid button-up and faded black slacks, his lace-up walkers whose toes showed wear. He clenched his fists. There was no avoiding Russell now. Walter put his head down until he knew he knew the two were close enough that avoiding acknowledgement was impossible.

"Walter."

"Russell," he mumbled, striding past Russell and wishing they were in an alley behind a bar.

"Say, Walter…"

Fuck, thought Walter. He hated it when people started sentences with "say"; it was a clear signal that whatever came next was going to be either a request or an admonition. He turned around. "Yeah, Russell."

"I just … well, I just wanted to know if you wanted to have a beer sometime. Sort this thing out. We do have to work together, after all."

Walter felt his cheeks heat up. He looked around to make sure no students were present and then looked Russell square in the face.

"No, Russell. I do not want to have a goddamned beer with you." He turned away, although now he was going the wrong direction.

"Walter, say—wait up."

"Damn it. What?"

Russell smiled, a serpentine grin—the kind he gave his students when they tested him in class.

"If you're curious, we could talk instead of you parking outside the house."

Walter closed his eyes and exhaled.

"What are you talking about?"

"Last night. Your Chevy. I think it was about ten-thirty or so."

"Wasn't me. Got better things to do."

"Sure. Well, Maureen said it sure looked like you and your car. Not the first time, either."

Walter rubbed his eyelids.

"You're fucking my wife," he said. Then he hurried past Russell and was out the door before Russell could get in another word.

*

At home, he made himself a small dinner and tried to settle into television, but he could take no comfort in plots tonight. He got out of his chair and walked into the garage. He plugged in the old refrigerator and stocked it with what beer was left in the house. He surveyed his surroundings: the bramble of unused tools and paint, the oil-stained floor, the calendar whose months had all passed unmarked. The whole room seemed like a museum; the only thing that had changed in years was the entrance and exit of his old Chevy, whose presence or absence mattered little.

He did not know what to do in the room or where to start. But he felt the urge to organize it, to throw out what was useless and create space for what was valuable. He began with the tools that were sitting out on his workbench: screwdrivers with heads of various sizes, handsaws, wrenches. He sorted the tools into piles and then began hanging them from the pegboard above the bench. After the top of the workbench was clear, he moved on to organizing his toolbox, and after that, the piles of wood that littered both far corners.

When they were first married, he had built Maureen several small things: a spice rack, a corner shelf, a nightstand. If Maureen even mentioned something in passing, he would build it for her, working tirelessly until the project was complete. Then as the years passed, he started projects but stopped finishing them: new closet doors, which still leaned against the back wall of the garage, a frame for a painting Maureen had bought at an antique store. As he surveyed the half-finished projects, he realized he could not explain why he had never finished them, why finally he had just stopped building anything at all. He picked up a piece of pine and ran his hand along it. A small splinter snagged his fingertip, which began to bleed. The blood spread onto the board, soaking into its capillaries. The red reminded him of Maureen's sweater from the night before. Some time before she left—presumably before the affair—she had asked him for one other thing: a red bookshelf. Something small and rectangular—longer than it was tall. She wanted it for her cookbooks and photo albums. He remembered listening to her neutrally, nodding his head, and then her request had slipped off into the air. Now, with the board in his hand, he wondered if fulfilling that small request would have made a difference at the time. He started thinking of *Tender is the Night*, a book she had told him to read, and wondered if he had become Dick Diver in the eyes of Maureen, a mad scientist full of failed attempts at husbandry.

Compulsively, he started digging through the wood. There was enough for a bookcase, more than enough, and it had been sitting here lifelessly all along. He dug through a drawer haphazardly until he found a carpenter's pencil and a piece of scratch paper. With a furrowed brow, he sketched a simple design and then calculated a formula for turning the drawing into the bookshelf Maureen wanted. He carefully measured the boards that would serve as the outside of the frame to create a rectangle wider than it was high. Then, using his old circular saw, he cut the boards to size. He glued together the wooden rectangle, holding it in place with bar clamps. As he screwed the frame together and removed the clamps, he did not think of Maureen or Russell or Dick Diver. He thought of nothing but the next task he needed to complete. Soon he marked the height of the shelves, having used a book on gardening Maureen left behind as a measure. He screwed L-brackets into place and then secured the shelves with extra screws. By the time the shelf was together, he had started sweating despite the minimal heat provided by the one small space heater in the garage. He paused for a moment, admiring his work, and then sanded the shelf. When it was smooth, he painted it cherry red, the color she had wanted. He put it near the space heater, switching the heater on high, so the hot air would make the shelf dry faster. His heart still racing with the frenzy of his activity, he sat in an old lawn chair and drank a can of beer.

By the time the shelf dried, midnight had just passed. He covered it with a ragged sheet, and then loaded it into the back of the Chevy, slipping on the patches of ice in the driveway and cursing while he did so. When he turned the corner onto Russell's street, the car fishtailed. He imagined Russell and Maureen in bed together, Russell's arm loose around Maureen's waist— the way his arm had been loose around it for years, and he wondered if once, just once, she had thought about him while turning over and letting Russell hold her, or if they talked about him, objectively discussing his failures as a husband and partner to Maureen, both of them pitying him, the things he could not do. Perhaps Maureen had made her famous spaghetti for dinner that night and they had drunk a bottle of Pinot Noir and watched a movie— probably something heady because that was Russell. And that was Maureen.

He pulled into the driveway, his headlights illuminating Russell's clean, white garage door. He put the Chevy into park and left the headlights on and the motor running. The porch light was on, and the house was a beacon in the dark cold. For a second, Walter swore he smelled Maureen as he carried the shelf to the doorstep.

He stood on the step for a minute and contemplated whether to ring the bell or whether to leave. He reached his finger out, feeling the smooth surface of the bell, but pulled it back. Then in a burst, he pushed the bell in, holding it steady for a second.

Almost immediately, a light flipped on in the front room, and he saw Maureen approaching. She opened the door wearing her pink flowered bathrobe, her eyes heavy with sleep.

"What are you doing here, Walter?"

Walter shuffled his feet in the newly accumulated snow. "I made this for you," he said, removing the sheet.

Maureen sighed heavily. "The bookshelf."

"The bookshelf."

"You remembered."

"Finally."

"You know it's too late."

"I know," he said, but a train announced its arrival, drowning out his words.

Maureen frowned and put a hand to her ear. Before he could repeat himself, her head whipped around, and Walter knew that Russell was behind her.

"It's fine, Russell," Maureen called over her robed shoulder. Russell said something Walter could not hear. Maureen gestured at him dismissively. She turned back toward Walter quickly, and to him, it seemed that she had moved closer.

Her eyes caught the light and Walter could see moisture collecting in them. She opened her mouth, but Russell was there before she spoke, and she straightened her posture, the distance between her and Walter growing again.

"Walter, what are you doing here? It's the middle of the night."

"I had to give her something I owed her."

"It's just something I left at the house. Something I wanted that was from a long time ago," Maureen said.

Russell smiled his serpentine grin. "How thoughtful."

"I was just leaving," Walter said.

"Sounds like a good idea." Russell touched Maureen's shoulder. "I'm going to go to the kitchen to pour us some milk," he said, and then walked away.

"Good night, Walter," Maureen said, but she did not turn away, not yet. She stood in the doorway, the light behind her spilling out over him.

"Good-bye, Maureen," he said, and then it was he who turned away toward the railyard, where the train that had rushed in a moment ago slowly crept down the tracks, and then paused, only to steal away again.

THE VINTAGE

Rose examined herself in the mirror. First, she looked at herself lengthwise, and then she looked at herself sideways, lifting up her shirt to reveal the large roll of flesh hanging over the elastic waistband of her pants. She pulled her breath in, but that made little difference. She had no delusions about the fact that she was no longer beautiful; she had not been beautiful for fifteen years. However, what she did not understand was how she had gotten so fat. Clever garments designed to slim and tuck could no longer hide the cascades of flesh on her trunk. She shook her head, walked away from the mirror, and uncorked another bottle of wine, a 2008 Cabernet Sauvignon from Dark Star Cellars in Paso Robles, California. Cabs were not her favorite, but because this was made in Paso Robles, she could not help but buy it. She poured just a little and then dipped her nose into the glass, inhaling the wine's rich and oaky scent. As it rolled around her palate, it changed—starting with fruit and ending with spice. This was just one reason she liked wine: it had the power to transform itself while still on the tongue.

She filled her glass and walked toward the living room where the couch waited expectantly, her blankets and pillows shaped like the beds deer make in cornfields. Just as she sat down to her watch her cooking program, the phone rang. She glanced at the cuckoo clock on the wall and shook her head. It was almost 10 p.m.

"Hello?"

"It's me."

"Mary, it's late. What's wrong?"

"Nothing's wrong."

"OK."

"I just wanted to say hello."

"Hello, sweetie. How are you?"

"Fine—Mom, I just wanted to call and tell you I'm OK."

Rose took a sip of her wine. "Have you been drinking?"

"Well, that's the pot calling the kettle black, isn't it?"

"Oh, Jesus, Mary."

Silence.

"Well, how's school?"

"School. Right."

"You *are* still going, aren't you?"

"You *are* still dieting, aren't you?"

"Why did you call if you were just going to act like this?"

"I'm sorry, Mom. Really. I didn't call to be difficult. I just wanted to say I'm doing OK."

"That seems like an odd reason to call. Did something happen? You can tell me—did you quit school again?"

"Nothing happened. Everything's fine. I'm always fine."

"Yes, you always have been fine."

Mary started laughing then.

"What's so funny?"

"Nothing. Nothing. I'm sorry. I just wanted to tell you I was fine and say good night."

"Good night, Sweetie. Love you."

Silence.

"Take care of yourself, Mom."

Then the line fell as silent as a country graveyard. Rose held the phone in her hand for a second, still half-expecting her daughter's voice to come back through it. After she hung it on the receiver, she tried to lose herself in her program. There was no doubt that Mary had been odd on the phone. More often than not, she did not even bother to call. It was Rose who always called her. It was Rose who maintained their relationship, however scant it was. Despite the oddness of the call, hearing Mary's voice on the line energized Rose, and as she took notes on a recipe for orzo with roasted vegetables, she imagined herself and Mary sitting down to dinner together, sharing a bottle of wine—perhaps a Pinot Grigio or a Riesling, which she knew Mary preferred, and chatting warmly like mothers and daughters were supposed to do. *Delicious. Simply delicious,* Mary would say. Having lost herself in her imagination, Rose soon fell asleep, and the sounds of food—peeling, chopping, sizzling—echoed in her dreams.

Several years ago, when the kids were teenagers and could largely care for themselves, she had taken to watching cooking and food programs. She watched shows in which men traveled to Third-World countries to eat savory bits of fresh kills—stomach and anus. She watched women with perfect teeth making ten-minute meals for families they did not have. She often tried the recipes that appealed to her, the TelePrompTer in her mind flashing descriptions of what she was doing as she did it. *Beat the egg whites until they form soft white peaks. Then fold them into the batter.* She was usually drinking while she created, and she thought of herself as an artist as she riffed on recipes, measuring with pinches and handfuls instead of tablespoons and teaspoons. Like wine, food came alive. It changed when she cooked it, the flavors intensifying with roasting and sautéing, the smells once caged behind skins set free. Food amazed her. Now when the table was set for one, and she served herself, she was usually just drunk enough so that whatever she made was perfect. *Delicious. Simply delicious,* the TelePrompTer said. Then neither the extra weight nor the fact that she was dining alone mattered.

It was only when her daughter Mary came over or called that she felt self-conscious about her weight. It was ridiculous to feel that way, she knew. Mary was her daughter, and parents did not answer to children. But every time they met, Mary's expression, which still reeked of both adolescent pride and rejection, told Rose that Mary was angry and that perhaps she would always be. She would not let go, not when her father and brother were somewhere in Paso Robles living in a temperate climate, and she and Mary were still in Minneapolis, each living alone, trying to keep an even keel despite the polarity of the seasons.

Rose woke up on the couch a few hours later to an infomercial for the Magic Bullet, a small electric blender *perfect for party drinks, salsas, and quick soups*. She had seen the commercial several times; several times, she had talked herself out of buying it, but this time she thought of using it to make guacamole, Mary's favorite, or broccoli cheese soup, another of Mary's favorites. She wanted that Magic Bullet. She picked up the phone and dialed the number on the bottom of the screen. A young woman chomping on a wad of gum answered the phone, called her "Hon," and took her credit number efficiently. When Rose hung up, she felt better, as though something she had been meaning to accomplish was complete. The Magic Bullet was on its way, and when it arrived, she would invite Mary over for party dips and margaritas, and they would sit on the couch and watch movies, something mothers and daughters were supposed to do.

After placing the order, Rose walked herself to bed. A few minutes after she lay down, she was falling into the bed, then through the bed, until she landed on the central coast of California. She was driving on Highway 64 through the hills of Paso Robles with her car windows rolled down, warm, damp air blowing through the car. Though it was still miles away, she could smell the ocean, and her stomach sang with the excitement the landlocked feel when they near it. In the distance, she saw vineyard after vineyard, grapes heavy on the vine. The sun was setting in its slow splendor, as music, effervescent and cinematic, came out from the stereo. Soon she was approaching a black iron gate, half an insignia on each side, and then she was being let through the gate, and then someone was opening her car door, then someone was handing her a glass of red wine—perhaps a Syrah or a Pinot Noir. When she turned around to look out over the vineyard, she saw him. After all this time, he was there.

Late the next afternoon, the phone rang.

"Is this Rose Mitchell?"

"Yes, can I help you?"

"I'm calling from Hennepin County Medical Center. Your daughter, Mary Mitchell, was in an accident. Can you come down?"

"Is she OK? What happened?"

"I'm sorry, ma'am. I don't have any more information."

71

Rose was silent for a moment. "Yes, I'll be right there," she said, her heart beginning to pump hard. She pulled on her undergarments, elastic things that gripped and raised, and then a pair of slacks and a blouse. Over the blouse, she pulled on a sweatshirt and then a long wool coat and scarf. She stuffed her slacks into winter boots and hurried through the mess of snow on her sidewalk. As she moved from the house to the car, she started imagining various scenarios—all of them starting with Mary and a bottle of vodka. She imagined blood running out of the corner of Mary's mouth and blood running out of her nose. She imagined Mary's eyes fixed and glassy, her body slumped over in the driver's seat of her beat-up Mazda, which had run off the road and into a tree. It was silent, and large, light snowflakes collected on the roof of the car and on the branches of the tree into which it had smashed. Rose drove faster.

Inside, the hospital the light was bright enough to make Rose squint. The nurses glowed with manufactured positivity while the doctors bustled around wearing glasses and furrowing their brows. Machines dispensed shitty coffee, and in the lobby people worried donuts down their throats. There was pacing and fidgeting, slow-motion magazine reading, superficial conversation. Clerical staffers on their breaks had donned tennis shoes and were getting their daily exercise in the hallway. Rose looked to her right and then her left and back to her right where a young woman with hair dyed such an intense black it looked blue stared at a computer screen.

"Hello?" she said. The woman raised her eyebrows in cool acknowledgement. "I got a call that my daughter was here."

"Name, ma'am?"

"Mary Mitchell."

After a long moment in which Rose stared at her, the woman handed Mary a card with a room number on it and pointed to a bank of elevators.

"Take those elevators to the fourth floor. Take a right when you get off the elevators and go to the end of the hall," she said in a voice as bored as data entry.

"Thanks," Rose said, but the woman was already reabsorbed into her computer screen.

When she arrived at Mary's room, Rose pulled the curtain back just inside the door and walked in. Mary's face was turned toward the television on which some talk show played. One of her legs was elevated and an IV was in her arm. She did not turn her head as Rose approached her. Rose pulled a chair up to the side of the bed and put a hand on Mary's shoulder, but Mary did not stir. Rose stared at her chest, making sure that it was still rising and falling rhythmically, holding her own breath until she saw evidence of Mary's. She exhaled, her hand growing heavier on Mary's shoulder. Mary shifted slightly and sighed. Tears welled in Rose's eyes, and she longed to squeeze

Mary's shoulder to pull her from wherever she was, but she did not allow herself to do it. Here now, in the rhythm of the hospital, she could sense Mary's truth, a truth she knew was dark, a truth for which she was probably responsible in some form. Mary could usually trace every problem she had back to Rose—bad skin, a poor metabolism, and a broken home that on its own was the mother of many other problems. Rose closed her eyes and exhaled. The TelePrompTer began. *All you have to do is combine all the ingredients in the short cup and twist on the cross blade. Then, just pulse a few times and voilà, guacamole!*

She remained that way for more than an hour, soothing her mind by cooking recipe after recipe as she remembered them from the Magic Bullet infomercial and other cooking shows, before Mary's eyes finally flitted open. When they stopped flitting, they widened in complete lack of recognition and then relaxed when she was aware of who was touching her. She shifted and Rose's hand fell off her shoulder.

"You're awake."

"How long have you been here?"

"Hour or so. I haven't even seen a nurse yet."

For a moment they were both silent.

"What happened?"

"It's a long story, Mom, and I'm tired."

"Jesus, Mary, you can't *not* tell me."

"It was nothing. I feel stupid about it now."

"*I* don't judge *you*."

"No, you don't. Not when you want something."

"Christ almighty. Just tell me what happened. We don't need to carry on this way."

"I fell, OK? It was stupid. It was a dumb thing. I fell down."

"In your apartment?" Rose asked, picturing Mary's dingy little apartment with its off-white walls and old sash-cord windows.

"Yes. In my apartment."

"What were you doing?"

Mary sighed loudly and began pulling on her blanket. When she raised her hand, Rose saw that it was trembling.

"Well?" Rose persisted.

"Decorating."

"Decorating? You've been in that apartment for two years."

"So? That doesn't mean I can't change things around."

"How did you fall exactly?"

"We can talk about it later," she said, wiping her nose with a shaking finger. "Listen—I need a favor. Can you go to my apartment and get some things?"

"Of course, but I want to know what happened. Can you just tell me that before I go?"

"Please, Mom. Not now. I'm fine. Just like I said last night. I'm fine. The knee will heal. They're doing the surgery early tomorrow morning."

"Fine," Rose said, as evenly as she could manage, but she knew a tone had slipped into her voice.

"You know what? Forget it. There's nothing that I really need."

"I said I'd go, Mary. Don't make this more difficult. What do you need?"

"My black pajama pants and a T-shirt. It's all in my bedroom. Then my makeup and toothbrush and face wash. That's all in the bathroom. My keys are in my purse over there." She gestured to a small closet.

Rose took the opportunity of having access to Mary's purse to rifle through it more slowly than she should have but did not see anything out of the ordinary.

"Did you find them?"

Rose held up the keys and jiggled them. "I'll be back soon," she said.

"Take your time. I'm not going anywhere."

"Right, sweetie. I'll see you."

After crossing the door's threshold, Rose stopped and looked back in the room. Mary's hand gripped the remote control, but her eyes were turned toward the window, and Rose imagined that she was far, far away. She wanted to rush back into the room, to embrace her daughter, but she knew the gesture would not be well received, and so she left, the keys bouncing in her pocket as she walked.

Mary's apartment was in Whittier, a neighborhood that epitomized not a melting pot but more so a rich tapestry. Christians, Muslims, Africans, Mexicans, hipsters, Vietnamese, Hmong—all of them populated the streets of Whittier. Mary's building was on the corner of Blaisdell and 28th Street, a long, dingy building where people came in and out at all hours. Rose had never understood why Mary insisted on living in the city when she could have had a quieter, more comfortable apartment in Brooklyn Park or Crystal or some other suburb. She walked in the front entrance where a few residents loitered, talking amongst themselves.

"Did you hear the ambulance?"

"Yeah—who was it?"

"I think it was that girl who lives up at the far end of the hall," a woman said, gesturing toward Mary's apartment, her large gold earrings swaying as she talked.

"You seen her come back yet?"

"Not yet."

"Shit. I wonder what happened."

Me too, Rose thought as she walked toward Mary's apartment, imagining the paramedics in their black slacks and jackets rushing into the apartment, knocking on the door, and Mary dragging herself to answer it. It amazed her just then, as her feet padded in the same steps that the paramedics' had earlier that day, the same steps her daughter routinely walked. *That really happened*, she thought.

Inside the apartment, the cream-colored standard-issue window blinds were all shut, and the air smelled of stale milk, the combination of the darkness and sour stink almost palpable. "Jesus Christ," Rose said aloud, immediately anxious and claustrophobic.

She opened the blinds, letting hard winter light flood the living room. Dishes littered the coffee and end tables. Dirty socks were rolled up and shoved into various corners. In the kitchen, more dishes were piled up haphazardly along the counter. She dropped her purse on the floor by the entryway; tears started to pool in her eyes, but she resisted them, forcing the TelePrompTer in her head to start. *Even with just a few simple ingredients, you can make a delicious home-cooked meal for your family.* As the TelePrompTer played, what she needed to do dawned on her. She needed to make something for Mary to eat. She would bring it to the hospital, and Mary would feel better— she would have to. Rose walked into the kitchen. Shriveled pieces of ground beef were crusted on dinner plates. Cloudy forks and spoons hid between bowls and plates. Mold floated atop a pan of uneaten spaghetti sauce. The remnants of waxy brown scrambled eggs sat in a skillet. Napkins tumbled out of the garbage can. Something dirty or decaying surrounded Rose everywhere she turned. There had to be alcohol somewhere in this place. She needed a drink. Finally, in the freezer, she found a half of bottle of vodka. In the refrigerator was a carton of orange juice. She checked the expiration date and then mixed herself a screwdriver in the only drink ware left in the cupboard— a coffee mug that read *The Big Apple* above a picture of New York City's skyline, the twin towers still standing stoically. It was a souvenir from the last trip they took as a family when Mary was a freshman in high school and Bobby a sophomore. Somehow, she felt guilty drinking out of it.

Maneuvering around the clutter, she rummaged through Mary's cupboards until she found some spaghetti noodles. There was flour in the cupboard, and milk, butter, cheap grated Parmesan, and a jar of minced garlic in the refrigerator. The milk was a couple days past its expiration date, but a day or two did not matter. She started to make a simple white sauce, something she always remembered Mary liking. Yes, she thought, this was how she would make things better. For a moment, she felt lifted, but when she wanted the happy hum of the TelePrompTer to play in her mind, it would not start. It was being in Mary's apartment that stopped it. In the truest place of her heart, she admitted that she did not like being in her daughter's

75

apartment. She loved Mary, but whenever she was in this apartment, she felt lonely and haunted, for she had cleared her own house of nearly all the memories of their time as a whole family. Pictures were packed away. Bobby's childhood things had been disposed of or put in the attic. Every trace of her ex-husband had been erased, but in Mary's apartment, specters loomed. Photos, gifts, and hand-me-downs were in nearly every room. Each time Rose stepped across its threshold, she felt as though she were stepping backwards through time. When she returned to her house in Brooklyn Park and the present, she always walked through the rooms just to make sure everything was as she had left it.

As she continued to sip from the New York mug, she started thinking about her ex-husband, Mary's father, which made her nervous. No matter how many times she reflected on their split, she could never quite pinpoint when they had begun leaving each other. It had happened in such small increments. By the time Mary was in the eighth grade and Bobby was a freshman in high school, Rose still had not gone back to doing secretarial work. Richard made enough and did not ask her to work, so she stayed at home, finding new ways to keep herself busy. Each day she woke with a to-do list penciled in her brain. Shopping. Cooking. Eating. The list was enough to distract her from whatever may have been happening between her and her husband and how she herself was changing. As the months turned into years, she had not noticed how much tighter her pants were growing, how much fuller her face was growing. She had not noticed that weeks easily went by in which she and Richard did not make love, though they shared several balanced dinners, each of which Rose presented with artfulness. She did not notice the books on winemaking, on California that her husband brought home, or that he had opened a new savings account. She did not notice that they had stopped talking except as talking related to the mundane activities of their daily lives. Despite all this, she supposed she was happy—or at least comfortable, which was far more than many people could ask for in life. So finally one night when he told her that he wanted to start a winery in Paso Robles, California, that he had found an old property for sale, one that he could afford, that he had done all the necessary research, she was shocked. She sat straight up in bed.

"Are you drunk, Richard?" she said.

"Of course not."

"Well, I don't know what to say."

"I have decided to go with or without you."

"What about the kids?"

"They're old enough to decide if they want to stay or go. Bobby will be eighteen in a year. Mary in less than two. They're old enough to make their own decisions."

"It's just that easy, is it?"

"Do you love me, Rose? Do you really?" he said on a note so biting that there would be no point in pretending.

"I suppose raising kids and all the years start to wear on you," she replied, clutching the top of the duvet cover on their bed, a slow panic creeping through her body.

Richard neither confirmed nor denied her statement. They both lay awake then, and she listened to him for any movement, any sigh or whisper, any sign that perhaps there was a way out. But he neither moved, nor sighed, nor whispered. Over the course of those next sleepless hours, Rose began imagining life without him, cutting him out of family photos, family trips. Next she cut out Bobby, and then it was just her and Mary, eating quiet dinners around the table, the noise of men removed from their house. Once she thought of it that way, the situation seemed tolerable—something, like a certain amount of poison, that her body could process and absorb.

"You can take Bobby but not Mary," she blurted out an hour or so after they had stopped talking. "You can't take both of them."

To her surprise, Richard turned over immediately. "I would never *try* to take both of them."

"Let's just agree right now then," she said. "You can have Bobby if you want, but leave Mary here. She's a girl. She belongs with her mother."

"Fine. I agree."

"How are we going to tell them?"

"We'll just do it."

"They're going to fight us."

"Bobby's going to want to go with his father."

Rose's instinct then had been to say, "And Mary will want to stay with her mother." But the words jumbled up, and she waited for Richard to say something like it, but he said nothing.

"So you think they'll be OK?" Rose said a moment later.

"You think they don't know how we've been living?"

She was silent because when she thought about it, she did not know what he had meant when he said *how we've been living*. She had not thought of it. Life had been too busy, but now that he said it that way, she suddenly pictured him at work, his job opening and closing accounts and helping customers at Wells Fargo. How many days he must have stared off into the brown fabric of his cubicle walls thinking of grapes and warmth. How many days must have passed on which young women sat down across from him and asked him for his help and advice, their skin innocent and pure, their bodies pert and full.

"Have you met someone else?" Rose asked, trying to hide any notes of jealousy.

Richard did not answer, and she could sense, from the habit of having shared a bed with him for over twenty years, that he was finally asleep.

What Rose remembered about the next two months was that everyone seemed to sleep too much, and if they were not sleeping, they paced and snapped like leashed dogs. By the time Richard and Bobby's things were gone, everyone looked older. Mary, Rose's precious Mary, who Rose had begun courting as soon as she knew divorce was imminent, only paid attention to her when Rose told her that she could go to California to visit her father on her own. Only then had Mary's eyes lit up and only then had Mary rushed toward Rose with open arms.

When Mary returned, her father called her often and she called him and Bobby often. As the months passed, the calls came less frequently and Rose did nothing to encourage them, refusing to broach the subject of her ex-husband and son. Mary began spending more of her time silently reading books about California late into the night, furtively drinking from the liquor cabinet until Rose was forced to put a lock on it, if not for Mary's sake then for her own because she could not afford to keep them both drinking. Soon the calls stopped altogether, leaving Mary listless and silent.

The heat from the electric stove made Rose sweat. Her blouse clung to the curves of her body awkwardly. As she sautéed the garlic, she opened the windows of the apartment to let cold air flood it, the redolence of rotting food replaced by garlic and the stiff, cottony odor of snow.

After the pasta was cooked to a perfect al dente and tossed with the sauce, Rose needed to use Mary's bathroom. As she walked through the living room, she noticed flecks of glitter catch the sunlight. There in the corner next to a five-gallon pail was a glittery jump rope. Rose recognized it from Mary's seventh birthday—the birthday they had spent at Lake Calhoun. She picked it up and inspected it in the light. It was completely ordinary, something any young girl would have delighted in receiving as a gift. But there was one thing about it that caught Rose's eye—between the handle and the rope on one side were pieces Mary's hair. They spun and shone in the light, wavy, and red. It didn't make sense to Rose—of all things, why would this be in the living room? Why the jump rope? Rose sat down on the pail, still holding it. On the floor, she noticed errant flecks of plaster. She looked up to see a wound, circular and deepening toward its center, in the ceiling's plaster. None of it made sense. There was no added décor, no evidence that Mary had been decorating. She gazed out the window where a black man in a heavy jacket and stocking cap held the hand of a small child. The child trailed slightly behind him wearing a blue jacket with mittens dangling from strings, a child who was already in love with the world. Suddenly the TelePrompTer that had abandoned her earlier kicked in. *The Magic Bullet is perfect for family gatherings! Make salsa and cheese dip on game day and root for your favorite team.* "Shut up!" she said aloud, silencing it.

She forced herself off the pail and into the Mary's dingy bathroom where she used the toilet sitting on her hands. When she had the food and everything that Mary had requested packed up, she looked back over the apartment one last time. Then, she went back and reached for the jump rope, which she wound around her hand and elbow and packed in her purse.

Back at the hospital, Mary, blurry-eyed, was watching *Wheel of Fortune*.

"Are you winning?" Rose asked, unconsciously asking a question Richard used to ask as a joke.

"Obviously," she replied without turning her head from the set.

"I thought maybe they'd get the piss and vinegar out of you in here."

"Tall order, Mom," Mary said, her voice loose and wet.

"I brought you some food. I made pasta with a garlic white sauce. Your favorite."

"It's not my favorite, Mom. It's your favorite. Besides, I can't eat now. Surgery's early tomorrow, remember?" she said, her eyes still fixed to the set.

"Sorry—I forgot. About the surgery I mean."

"It's fine."

"Will you stop watching the TV and look at me?"

"Jesus. What?" Mary said, the same looseness in her voice. She dropped the remote control and turned toward Rose.

Rose sat down and folded her hands in her lap. She exhaled, preparing herself for whatever winds might come. "I want you to tell me something honestly, OK?" She paused. "I want you to tell me what you did to yourself in that apartment."

"What I did to myself? I told you. I had an accident. I was trying to decorate and I fell."

Rose pulled the jump rope from her purse and held it out to Mary. They locked eyes, the silent rope between them.

"Trying to decorate with what? With this? What were you going to hang it from the ceiling? I saw the plaster on the floor," Rose said.

"I just asked you to bring me a few things."

"And I did that. Now I'm just asking you a question and asking you to answer me honestly."

"Right."

"What?"

"You don't get to march in here and do this."

"Do what?"

"Guest star mom."

"Guest star mom? What are you talking about?"

"You want to know the real reason why you're here?" Mary said, her voice tightening. "You're here because you feel sorry for yourself."

"I don't know what you're talking about. I'm here because I'm worried about you. Mothers take care of their children."

79

"The same reason you let Dad leave with Bobby and kept me here. Because you wanted to take care of your daughter? A lot of good that did."

"I was good to you, Mary Marie. I *am* good to you, Mary Marie. I was there for anything you needed." Rose was standing then, surprised by her own anger, her purse dropping to the floor, keys and wallet spilling onto the tiled floor. "You didn't want for anything. I took care of you."

"Did you really?" Mary said, leaning forward in bed. "Or was it the other way around? Because I certainly remember putting you to bed more nights than you put me to bed. All the wine, the wine tastings, and the cooking classes that always involved wine. All the times I picked you up."

"I don't have to listen to this." Rose's face was flushed and her heart was pounding. She stooped over and struggled to pick her keys up off the floor.

"Not easy to reach your feet, huh?"

Rose paused, bent over, the keys just out of reach.

"I was a good mother to you. I *am* a good mother."

"Tell yourself whatever you need to."

"I don't have to listen to this garbage anymore," Rose said, nearly falling over as she finally reached the keys. She walked toward the door and bumped into a nurse on the way out.

At the elevators, she jammed a thick finger into the down button repeatedly until one arrived. Walking out of the hospital, she shot a dirty look at the woman she had talked to earlier. On the way home, she drove the same way Richard used to when he was angry: jaw wired shut, yellow lights sped through as they turned red, corners taken hard and fast. Children were not supposed to question parents. Who was Mary to question her? Rose knew she had been a good mother. As she stared down the glowing path created by her headlights, she began trying to remember how she had taken care of Mary when Richard and Bobby left. But all she could remember were green bottles through which different hues of red caught the light in the kitchen. She could remember pouring wine, inhaling its scent—wooden and spicy—and examining its legs. She could remember searching, as Mary's footsteps padded around her, searching for the perfect vintage.

DINNER WITH EDWARD

The first time she sees him, Loretta stops in the middle of the street, her hands so tight on the steering wheel that blood drains from her knuckles. Beads of sweat gather underneath her arms, above her lip, and in the crack between her lower lip and chin. When she tries to swallow, she cannot gather enough saliva. Out of myth, he is suddenly there. He looks the same, she supposes, except that he is dirty and his thinning hair has grown even thinner. A car honks, startling her, and she starts driving, unable to help herself from circling around again. He sits in Washburn Fair Oaks Park on a bench along the only path that runs through it, a diagonal walk that opens to the Minneapolis Institute of Arts on one end and the Gale Mansion on the other. What lies between is part wasteland, part alleyway—a haven for the wandering. In winter, it is especially desolate. Heavy, wet snow clings to the oaks. The only things except for Edward and the trees that dot its grim landscape are the sparrows and squirrels scavenging in the snow. *So this is where he has made his home*, she thinks. She watches as he rips a small corner off the gas station sandwich in his hand, the white bread stark against his dark jacket. He throws part of it to a squirrel and another part of it to a cluster of sparrows. Loretta wants to go home right then and tell herself that it is okay to let go, now, now that she knows he has food and a jacket.

When she gets home, she cannot stop thinking of him alone with his cardboard sandwich, something she knows he hates—or would have hated before. *But that's not Edward*, she tells herself. *Not him, not Edward, not him, not anymore.* The image of him in the park will not leave her when she tries to sleep, and she spends most of the night with the sheets in a tangle around her restless limbs.

When the alarm goes off, she is still tired. She does not feel like teaching freshman comp today, a course hated amongst the faculty at Hamline University. Her section this semester is especially tiresome. It is split down the middle: athletes who care nothing for language, who despite their finely tuned bodies lack grace, and arrogant 18 year olds who believe either that they know everything about writing or that they do not need to know anything about it. This is the only class in which her mind wanders, in which she finds herself glancing at the clock. She moves around the room by rote, asking the same questions and selling the same ideas at every class meeting. *What is the thesis of this piece? Who can tell me? Come on; let's just start throwing out some ideas. Tom?* Some days she wants to scream at them the same way she imagines Edward had wanted to scream at his students. *It's not that damned difficult,* she wants to yell. But now she treads around them coolly with a forced patience so genuinely executed that the students do not detect in the slightest the edge she feels whenever in front of them.

She dismisses class a few minutes early and sees Blake, an old English professor who had been a friend of Edward's. She looks down at the papers in her hands and starts rearranging them in what she hopes will appear to be a meaningful way, but Blake has spotted her and he stops her just short of her office door.

"So, any word?" he says. His voice is barely above a whisper.

For a moment, she thinks about telling him what she saw in the park. Blake does not know, however, just how ill Edward had gotten before he left. Loretta would never have done that to Edward, would never have told his friends. He had not accepted her help when he started breaking down, and a man like him surely would not have accepted help from someone in academia, not after having lost his place in it. Her face flushes, and she looks down at her papers again.

"No, no word," she says, taking a half step back toward her office.

Blake shakes his head, and rubs his white beard in grandfatherly confoundedness. "You'll let me know, right?"

"Of course," she says, her eyes focusing on a spelling error in one of the essays. "But it's been a long time. I think he would have called by now if he had any plans to come back. Wherever he is, I'm sure he's fine. Hopefully happy." The ease with which she spits out the last two words surprises her.

"It's so strange. Just to leave like that," Blake says, which he says each time they see each other now.

"I know, Blake. I know."

"But he may come back around after he gets himself figured out. Don't give up hope just yet. Even Job kept hope."

"Right. Job," she says, crossing the threshold of her office.

On Highway 94, the traffic makes Loretta edgy and angry. She gets lost in her thoughts, as it stops and starts around her. She is thinking of the ruse she just constructed for Blake; she is telling herself that she needed to lie. To lie or to walk away before the conversation even started. Why couldn't she just walk away? How easy it had been for Edward to simply step out into the streets of Minneapolis and pull the door shut behind him without looking back. As she continues driving, she begins trying to think *through* Edward, as she has tried before. It is always difficult; after all, she has never lost a teaching job due to budget cuts, nor has she ever suffered intense periods of writer's block. She has found herself in creative deserts before, but once she started traversing them, she soon found her way back. What she imagines now about Edward is this: the burden of joblessness and artlessness had become too heavy to bear, so he baptized himself in a void, walking away with only his clothing, severing all commitments except those to his own body. Now he worries about survival, the gut. In that struggle, she imagines he is free. He does not have to think anymore, not like he had been thinking, his thoughts racing for hours and hours so that nothing could calm him, an unfathomably deep dark blinding him to what was actually happening in the world around him.

It still just hurts, though, that it was not by her hand, which she had offered so many times, but by the rejection of her hand that he had gained his freedom.

She realizes she has missed the Riverside exit and is heading west toward the center of Minneapolis. She steers her Honda onto the 11th street exit but does not say to herself, *I am going to drive by the park*. She says, *I am going to go downtown, I am going to go to the Art Institute, I am going to go to…I am going to go to…* But that is not true: within minutes, she is circling the block looking for him.

This time he sits on a bench at the Gale Mansion end of the park. His head hangs low, reminding her of the nights he would fall asleep sprawled out in the recliner in the living room of their house. Though her window is raised, Loretta reaches her hand toward him and imagines waking him up from one of those sleeps. His hair and face would be warm, his lips slightly parted so that she could see his teeth, teeth she had always envied, white and straight. A police car driving by flips on its siren and Edward turns his head. For a second their eyes meet, which startles her. She looks at him just long enough to know that he has not come back yet from wherever he has gone. *Edward,* she thinks, *you old ghost.*

Back at her one bedroom in Seward, she wades through essays about mothers and fathers, compositions littered with trite and shallow details, comma splices, fragments, and awkward constructions. She begins to think that she must be an awful teacher because good teachers' students obviously would not write terrible papers. Then she remembers a comment a good teacher had once given her on an essay: *Loretta, your essays are a bright spot in an otherwise dark world. Thanks! Prof. Johnston.* That was the only time she had ever imagined that the other students were not writing brilliant, insightful essays, far better than those she had worked on meticulously. On nights like these, she misses Edward. Some nights they had both graded so many papers that they were loopy by the end and could do nothing but drink whiskey and collapse on one another. Imagining it, she wants to lie down silently but does not have the time, not now, not when there is so much to be done. With renewed fervor, she reads and comments on the essays, reminding herself to write at least one good thing on each poor essay and to praise highly each well-written essay.

After the last paper is graded, she drops the stack on the floor by the side of the bed. The thud they make is satisfying. She turns off the light. When she retreats into the deepest cave of sleep, she will dream of Edward.

She will see him as he used to be before something broke in him and he could no longer teach, write, or be her husband. He will smile at her and speak to her cryptically as is the speech in all dreams. The weather will be warm; there will be no snow. The fair oaks will shade them, the breeze turning the oaks' leaves into song. She and Edward will be sitting together on a blanket, the soft blue blanket printed with tiny red flowers that they used to sleep under in their marriage bed. Edward will be smiling, his head tilted slightly, and the secrets of the married will be on their faces. *Eat*, he will say, *eat. I packed this just for you. Eat.* Then, as she is about to take the simple food prepared by his hand, she will wake, thirsty and hungry.

The morning arrives early and petulant. The dream hangs on her shoulders like an ill-fitted shirt. She eats dry toast and drinks ice water, all the while still living in the dream, not in the center of the dream, but in the outskirts of the dream, the part where she is a merely a spectator—one who knows she has just witnessed a farce. She repeats to herself that the dream is just that, but still it stays with her, and she lets herself indulge for moments at a time. As part of this indulgence, she drives to the grocery store and the liquor store before going to school. She buys Honeycrisp apples, the last of the season; smoked Gouda, their favorite brand; a fresh baguette; a bottle of cabernet, their favorite wine. She brings everything into her office and arranges it all carefully into one paper bag, which she stashes beneath her desk, feeling better just knowing it is there.

In class, the students workshop exemplification essays. When she had given them the prompt based on an essay about racism—write about a time when someone assumed something about you that was not true—they had all just stared at her. Now their papers show it, and she blames herself. She knows class will be painful, but she tries to remain upbeat. She picks one of the strongest writers to workshop first, trying to motivate the class. Once the student starts reading the first paragraph of his essay, she hears whispering from one side of the circle. Tom, a student who entered her class with 18-year-old arrogance, keeps talking to the person next to him. They snicker, their glances gesturing at the student reading. Loretta launches a frigid glare in his direction, and he stops whispering but continues to wear the same pompous grin he has all semester.

"Good, thank you," she says when the student finishes reading. "Now, I want to open this up to everyone. What did you like about the essay? Anyone. What did you like?" The room remains as still as a painted ocean. "Okay. I'll start," she says, struggling to keep frustration out of her voice. "I think the detail in these examples was very well done. I could picture the way people treated him when they found out about his sister's illness. I could see the looks on their faces—what was it he wrote, 'like I was marked'? Great line. Somebody else, somebody else. What did you like in the essay?"

As a few other students start commenting, Tom goes back to whispering. Each time he breaks from a whisper, he makes eye contact with Loretta as if to openly defy the classroom's order. She shoots him the same cold gaze, but he just continues talking. She holds her tongue, keeping him in her peripheral, until the wave of comments recedes.

"Tom," Loretta says, just as he is again turning toward the student next to him, "what did you like about this essay?"

"What?" he asks, still wearing the same grin.

"I asked you what you liked about the essay."

"Oh. Right. I wrote some comments, but they're not really in that category."

"That category?"

"Yeah. The let's-pat-each-other-on-the-back category."

Loretta can feel every muscle in her body heat and tense. She pauses and takes a breath before responding. "Well, Tom, presuming you actually did do the assignment and did it correctly, you should have written at least one thing in that category," she says, making air quotations around the words *that category*. All rustling of papers and shifting in seats halts. "Well?" Tom still stares at her, but now his smile is gone, and his jaw has started to pulse. She stands up and turns around, leaving her spot in the workshop circle for one behind the lectern. She perches herself there and leans forward, her eyes dead on Tom. "Hmm…No response. Tom, I am particularly fascinated that out of everyone in this class, you have no response. It is truly remarkable. Next time, if you don't feel like participating, don't bother coming." She gazes defiantly him, the class caught between them. "Take a break, everyone. Come back in 15."

When class resumes, Tom does not come back, and she does not know whether to feel proud or ashamed. What she does feel is unburdened, as though she just set down a very heavy bag. For the rest of the class, she avoids looking at Tom's empty chair and struggles to maintain what focus she has left. Afterwards, she pulls the door of her office shut behind her and leans back against it. She ignores the blinking message light on her phone, pulls the paper bag from beneath her desk, and quickly walks out with her head down so that no one will stop her in the hallway.

As Loretta starts her car, she can see Tom's face, alive with anger, and she wonders where he went when he did not return. His not returning gnaws at her as she wades through 94. He had been disrespectful, but she did not like losing her temper in class. The teacher is always supposed to remain calm. By the time she reaches the Riverside exit, her exit, all she can think of is how badly she wants to tell Edward what happened. He would know exactly what to say. She cannot help herself; she passes the Riverside exit, taking the 11th Street exit instead and driving to the park. She circles it, worried that Edward might not be there at all. Then she sees him sitting on a bench in the middle of the park, right along the sidewalk. He looks the same as he had the other day—his head tilted forward as if he is sleeping. A layer of snow is accumulating on his hair and Loretta imagines brushing it off with her fingers. She gets out of her car and walks toward the sidewalk that runs through the park, the snow packing easily beneath her feet. As she nears the bench where Edward sits, she imagines putting her hand gently under his chin and pulling his face up so that she can look into his eyes. When she imagines his eyes though, she does not see the eyes of the man she loves. Rather she only sees those of the man who left her, hollowed eyes that only yesterday had looked but failed to see.

Thinking of them, she stops, and instead of continuing to walk toward him, she walks across the park, finding a bench behind a tree. From the bench, she can watch him. She can imagine that he is sleeping, that she is just waiting for him to wake up to come to dinner. She opens the paper bag and begins taking out the contents. When she bites into the apple, she is back in the center of the dream, which is boundless. In the center of the dream, Edward wakes and crosses the park. He sits down next to her and reaches into the bag. He rips apart the baguette and cuts off a thick piece of cheese, a peculiar smile on his face.

Eat, he says, *eat.* She takes the food from him and smiles back. *So, what's on your mind?*

I blew up at a student today.

Well, did he deserve it? he says, smiling and nudging her.

Yeah. I guess he did. He was laughing at another kid's writing.

There you go, he says. *Then you don't need to worry about it. Sounds like he needed to be put into place.*

But he didn't come back to class after break, Edward. He just walked out and didn't come back...

A trickle of cold water runs down Loretta's neck, which pulls her back into the outskirts of the dream. She wipes the back of her neck with her hand, and runs a hand through her hair, melting the snow that has gathered in it. The paper bag at her side has grown damp, and she thinks about leaving, but then she remembers the wine. She uncorks the bottle and pours some into a paper cup. The cabernet is dry and rich and after a few sips, the cold begins to flee her bones.

She looks over at Edward, who has not moved. "Cheers, Edward," she says.

Then the dinner is over.

At home, she stares out the window into the purple darkness. Snow is still falling, but it has grown lighter and the flakes tumble in the wind. Another set of papers waits for her, a pen poised on top of them. She doesn't want to look at them, not now. She is tired of unending work. She is tired of the one bedroom, of Blake, of Tom. She is tired of missing Edward. *It would be so easy*, she thinks. She imagines pulling on her boots and long wool coat, wrapping a scarf around her neck. She imagines opening the front door, which always sticks a little, and shutting off the light. She imagines turning around and taking one last look over her dark apartment. She imagines the glow from the clock on the stove shining in the kitchen, and the streetlight casting a garden of slanted light on the hardwood floor. And then she imagines pulling the door shut behind her and stepping out into the snow.

APRON ON, APRON OFF

Percy did not normally attend craft fairs. He was, after all, a man. But his wife, now six months dead, had attended them regularly. So it did not feel strange when he entered the VFW on Lyndale Avenue upon seeing the "Craft Show Here TODAY!" sign outside. He walked down the asbestos-tiled stairs to the basement, which was abuzz with sellers and their wares. Long brown tables were arranged in streets and avenues, and he strolled through the neighborhoods, hands in the pockets of his flat-front khakis. Every so often he stopped when he saw something Bonnie would have liked. The first stop he made was in front of a cylindrical cloth bag designed to store plastic bags. The bag came in many patterns: tiny angels, Hawaiian flowers, plaid. He ran his fingers up and down the length of the heavy cloth.

"It makes the kitchen so much neater," the woman working the table said. She smiled at him, her eyes pinched so that her whole face hung from her temples. She had unnaturally red hair, and Percy let go of the bag as soon as she spoke to him. "Don't you have that problem," she said, "too many bags and nowhere to put them, so they're all over the place? Let me show you some more patterns. I probably have one to match your kitchen."

Percy stared at her. He processed the words at half the speed she had spoken them. Had Bonnie complained about plastic bag storage? He remembered a drawer in the kitchen that had been chronically jammed, a loss of usable space. In a fit of anxiety, he racked his brain trying to remember if he had fixed it or not. He could see the drawer; he could feel himself tugging at it—and then nothing. He cursed himself and slipped off before the woman turned around to bring out the other samples.

He passed over some booths he did not think Bonnie would care about—young stuff, feather earrings and other garish jewelry—stopping again when he got to a table full of nothing but aprons. There were aprons in every incarnation and print, some bodice-less with straight skirts, some with full bodices and ruffled skirts. They reminded him of dresses. Although as lovely, they were not dresses, which gave him license to do something men are rarely allowed to without arousing suspicion: with his thumb and forefinger, he began tasting the different patterns, savoring the stitching, lingering over the textures. He could picture Bonnie modeling each one of them with a shy smile and a hand on her hip. When he came out of his reverie, he was face to face with a woman at least twenty years his senior. Her hair was pulled back in a severe bun; she wore an apron of course, printed with tiny pale green and cream flowers, over a pale green dress. Her hands were crossed in her lap and she stared off into the artisan melee. He edged down the table, waiting for her to turn and attack. He was almost directly in front of her by the time she said, "Twenty dollars for a half and thirty for a full." Still she did not look at him. The schoolboy in him, still hanging there by a frazzled cord, was tempted to pass a palm in front of her face, to stick his tongue out at her and see if she noticed, but he wouldn't do that because the aprons were good enough— unlike much of the other tacky glued junk—that he felt awed by the table. His Bonnie, Bonita by given name who was six months dead, would have loved them.

"You buying, kid?" the woman asked.

"Does looking cost?"

"I'm seventy-five years old, kid. Everything costs."

He was a little thrilled by being called "kid."

"OK. I'm buying. What would you pick out for a woman named Bonita?"

"Bow-neeta?"

"It's Spanish for beautiful. Her father was half-Mexican."

"Bow-neeta. I'll be goddamned." She was still staring out over the crowd. "Bow-neeta."

He was shocked by her lack of helpfulness. "The woman over there with the bag holders was ready to come to my kitchen and custom match."

The woman laughed. "Let me know if you want to buy something, kid."

Percy scoffed at her to himself. Then, with schoolboy resilience, he resumed his surveillance, walking up and down the table and touching what he pleased. Even though Bonita was dead, he bought small things he thought she would like. She had been the kind of woman who even from the beginning of courtship elicited gifts from her suitors. He imagined it had started as early as grade school—flummoxed boys clustered around her, dandelions or chocolate in their grimy little hands. He had been and still was just one of them. Last week he bought her a pair of salt and pepper shakers, terriers of some sort whose black noses had magnets in them so that they were perpetually kissing. It made him feel better having those things in the house, like she was going to walk through the back door at any moment, put her arms around his neck and kiss him, her face aglow. *For me? Oh, pudding cup, you shouldn't have!* she would say, which was what she had always said when he brought her a gift. She would take the trinket in her hands, admire it briefly, and set it down where it would sit for perhaps a day or two before disappearing. Where the trinkets went he never knew, but he imagined she kept them somewhere secret and safe, somewhere so private that only she would ever see them.

There was one gifted trinket, however, that remained on display in the house. It was a small glass paperweight with a picture of the London Eye in it that Percy's coworker Charles had given her off-handedly one night at a company party. He had just returned from a trip there, which he all too eagerly blathered on about to anyone who would listen. Percy still remembered watching the transaction in his peripheral vision. Charles had held up one finger as if to say, *Just a minute.* Then he had reached into his leather attaché case and pulled out the paperweight. Bonita's eyes had lit up as if to say, *My goodness, Charles, this is so sweet of you!* The paperweight had rested on top of Bonnie's desk, never gathering dust. Shortly after the funeral, Percy seized it in a fit of grief and threw it in the garbage, replacing it with a black ceramic cat figurine he had bought for her.

Finally, he chose three aprons: one was a half with a light blue skirt populated by red and yellow flowers; another was a full with two pockets, a hyacinth print, and a ruffled border; and the final apron, the sexy one of the three, was a full that had a black, red, and white swirling flower print, black ties, two black pockets, and two black seams running up the skirt.

"Here," he said, slapping down $80 in front of the woman.

"Thanks, kid," she said, finally turning toward him. She took the money and stashed it in one pocket of her apron while gathering his prizes with her other hand. When she had gathered them all, she finally looked at him. "Tell Bow-neeta to come back and see us sometime."

Percy put two fingers to the top of his forehead, then pointed them at her and walked away, still hearing the old woman cackle and mumble.

On his way home, he drove down 28th Avenue by Lake Nokomis. It was February. The trees were white and perfect. The lake was white and perfect. The roofs of the one-and-half-stories were white and perfect. As he drove, he took his hand off the wheel and ran it over one of the aprons—the one with hyacinth print. It was the kind of apron she would have worn on a Saturday morning. On Saturday mornings they had made breakfast together, scrambled eggs with various themes—Mexican, Mediterranean, Spanish—hash browns made from raw Yukon gold potatoes with tiny chopped onions and garlic, and wheat toast. When the meal was ready, they feasted, lingering at the table in comfortable silence. During those mornings, he remembered feeling what he could only describe as content. He did not want. He would not have described himself in any sort of mood; rather, he just *was* and simply *being* was fine. The food, his wife's presence, the routine of their days sustained him. In the six months since her death, however, that feeling had fled him, and now each day he had to pay attention to mountains and valleys of emotions and desires—this moment hungry, this moment nauseous, and this moment thirsty, this moment drowning.

He turned right on 54th Street and drove forward until he came to 30th Avenue. On 30th Avenue, he turned left. He parked in front of his house, a Craftsman bungalow—the only one in the neighborhood—and turned off his Honda. He always forgot that he could park in the garage now. Bonita was not there, so he no longer had cause for that chivalry. When he realized he had done it again, he shook his head and rubbed the bridge of his nose with his thumb and forefinger, wondering if it would ever stop. Thinking about moving the car made him tired, so he picked up the aprons and walked inside. The reliable smell of the house greeted him—a cordial mixture of chocolate chip cookies and clean laundry—that remained unchanged despite Bonnie's departure.

After taking off his shoes, he crossed the living room, stopping to try to close the door to the hall closet, which had recently quit shutting even though he had fixed it at least three times. He could still imagine Bonnie, clad in a black skirt and red sweater with curlers in her hair, shoving the door shut and mumbling *Christ*. He shook his head, set the aprons down on the table, and pulled open the door to the new stainless steel refrigerator he had purchased after Bonnie passed. They had been planning to buy it before she died, and so after, he thought it only best to carry through with their plan. He surveyed its contents. There was not much: leftover mixed vegetables, a sure-to-be-dry chicken breast, a loaf of bread refrigerated to stave off mold, and some bottles of beer. He sighed and pulled out what was left of the food and set it on the table. Right now he imagined Charles was probably sitting down to a feast of ethnic food he had prepared himself. He was the kind of man who knew what *garam masala* was and who could make homemade paneer. Percy was glad Charles had stopped calling. He cracked a bottle of beer and took a long pull. It was cold and slightly bitter, hoppy, the way he preferred it. "Cheers," he said aloud to himself, staring at the aprons and wondering which one Bonnie would have picked up first.

On impulse, he grabbed the black and red one. He held it in front of himself and looked it up and down; then he pinched the seam, running his fingertips down its entire length. He had read a book as a kid, *Apron On, Apron Off*, and in it everyone had special aprons for specific tasks. When they put on the aprons, they were suddenly different somehow, ready to perform their duties—setting type, baking bread. He pulled the apron over his head and tied it around his back smoothing it with his palms. *Apron on*. He put the chicken and vegetables into one bowl and heated them in the microwave. He sat at the kitchen table, still wearing the apron, and picked at the second-rate food, loosening the knot in his throat with beer. As soon as his appetite had come, it was gone. He got up, washed the dishes, and put them away in their designated spots. He paced around the kitchen, straightening and tidying and clearing away any crumbs or dust he found. Finally, when there seemed nothing else to do, he untied the apron. *Apron off*.

He took the aprons upstairs and stretched them out on Bonnie's side of the bed. He examined the stitching on the black and red apron. It was even and neat, skilled, and it was hard for him to imagine that the woman who sold him the aprons was the one who created them. He was just about to turn out the light when something caught his eye. A piece of the duvet cover was visible through one of the apron's seams. He snatched it up and examined it more closely. There in the seam on the hyacinth print was a tear. For the length of an inch, the ruffle was disconnected from the skirt. He put his finger in the hole and watched it wiggle through. When he slid his finger the length of it, more of the stitching came out and the hole grew twice as long. He stared at it for a moment in disbelief. He could hear the old woman's mocking voice, *Bow-neeta*. He could hear her unwarranted, infuriating cackling. "That old witch," he said aloud. Then searching his pockets, he looked for a receipt or a card, but there was nothing. Had there been a sign on the table? He tore at the aprons, flipping them over, looking for any clue of who their maker was. Finally, he found a tag on one of them, the print so small that he had to squint to read it. *Aprons by Emily*, it said. Beneath the name was a phone number with no area code. He glanced at the clock. 10 p.m. The time did not matter. He did not care if he woke up that old witch, or her husband, or whomever she had convinced to live with her. With the aprons clenched in his fist, he went downstairs to the kitchen where a black telephone interrupted the wall by the microwave. He began typing in the number with different area codes in front of it: 612, 651, 763, 952, Minneapolis, St. Paul, northern suburbs, southern suburbs. No one answered at any of the numbers; at all but one, an answering machine clicked on announcing family names, some of them with children's voices trembling with the excitement of being recorded. Finally, he tried one last area code on a whim: 507. The phone rang and rang, and he imagined what the ringer sounded like in the house in which it resonated. He imagined the looks on the faces, the waiting to see who would finally get out of his or her chair to end the sound. Then someone picked up.

"Hello?" he said.

A throat cleared on the other end. "Hell-o," the person—a woman— said, accentuating the first syllable long past what was necessary.

"Is this *Aprons by Emily*?"

"Who is this?"

"I bought three aprons from you at a craft fair this afternoon. I gave you $80. You were rude, which I could probably look past, but one of the aprons is torn. I did not pay for a torn apron."

"*Bow-neeta's* husband, is it?"

"Yes," he paused, "yes, this is."

"So you want a new apron? I don't give refunds. It's on the back of the tag."

Percy turned the tag over like the page of some tiny book. In all caps, there it was—NO REFUNDS. "If that's the best you can do, then yes, that's what I want."

"I'm not going to be in the Twin Cities for a while now, kid. I don't do many events in the winter. Too hard driving through all that crap."

"I don't mind driving. I will come to you. Where are you located?"

"Rochester."

"Rochester?"

"Yes, kid, ever hear of the Mayo Clinic?"

"I know where Rochester is. I just didn't think you were going to be that far away."

"You didn't know what 507 meant?"

"Yes, sorry."

"You can wait until I come back thataway, but it won't be for another two months or so at least."

Percy thought about the apron sitting there, ripped, for two months. He hated the idea. He had never been able to stand the sight of things that were ripped, torn, or broken. That was part of the reason Bonnie had loved him. He never let anything in their house or their cars remain in disrepair for too long. First, he would try to fix whatever it was himself. He was not afraid of doing things on his own. Over the years he had acquired a garage full of tools all based around jobs that had needed to be done around the house. Wrenches and snakes for plumbing, ladders and rollers for painting. He liked the research and planning that came with each project, and he went into each fresh and hopeful with the blind confidence of a child. But more often than not, once in the middle of the job, he found himself perplexed by something he hadn't planned for properly, complications of living in an old house with old-house pipes and old-house wires. When he had mulled over the situation, called friends, and consulted the hardware store, which sometimes took weeks, he called someone else to finish the job. When the repair people came, he stayed close, watching them work, occasionally handing them tools, and talking—in industry terms—about the job. Since he stayed so close to the work, he still felt proud as if he had completed it himself. Bonnie would invite her friends over to show them the changes. *Work's all done. Oh yes, Sue, he does take good care of me.* Then more quietly, *Only took a month and a handyman's help to be able to use my own bathroom sink again, but it's done.* The women would smile at each other, co-conspirators, and shake their heads in the vague way women did so that he never knew exactly what they were thinking.

Despite all the times he had taken good care of her, of their house, he could only remember the one time he had failed her. It had been in the summer when the grass in their lawn seemed to grow inches each day. Maintaining the yard was his job, but their riding lawn mower had broken. He took it apart but could not put it back together again. Work at HealthPartners, the insurance company where he reviewed claims, had been busy—so many illnesses and surgeries, so many claims to review. He had simply forgotten to have someone fix the mower, simply not realized how high the grass had gotten, simply not realized that the neighbors had probably been shooting Bonnie looks when she came and went, simply not realized ....

"Fine. I'll come there."

"OK, kid. I'll see you tomorrow then."

"No, I'm coming now." He was sure he could not stand looking at the ripped apron when he woke in the morning—if he could sleep at all with it in the house.

The woman was silent for a second. "Suit yourself," she said and gave him the address.

"OK," he said, realizing after he hung up that the last word he said was not a closing, but an affirmation.

Outside, snow was falling. High, light flakes rushed the windshield with mesmerizing speed, making Percy feel as though he were driving through time itself. But tonight time didn't matter. He did not plan to go to work the following day. Since Bonnie died, his coworkers at HealthPartners did not bother him too much. They treaded lightly around him and did not question him when he called off, which he had done several times. There was no judgment in their voices when they inquired about claims he had approved, having reviewed them and either missed or ignored potentially damning details—pre-existing conditions, experimental procedures, visits to out-of-network physicians. He played the dolt when these errors were called to his attention, but the truth was that he no longer cared. Denying claims now seemed futile and ridiculous—almost laughable. In the face of life's unpredictability and brevity, who cared about one office visit to an out-of-network doctor? Who cared whether someone was allowed to have an experimental surgery? The cold, editorial eye he had once cast on claims had warmed and blurred so that he no longer saw pieces of paper but small lives. Bonnie's life had been one such small life.

At first after Bonnie died and his children went back to their homes in other cities, his coworkers had invited him over to their houses; they had given him hot dishes and casseroles in white ceramic pans, but then of course, all too soon, the invitations tapered off. There was only one man who kept checking in on him—Charles. To Percy's knowledge, Charles and Bonnie had only met a handful of times, one of which was at the company party where Charles had given her the paperweight. Still Charles kept calling long after the other calls had stopped, inquiring how Percy was, how Bonnie's family was, how their children were. At first, Percy enjoyed the calls, but when they didn't stop, he began to feel uneasy. Charles's grief (Percy often heard him choke up while they talked) seemed strangely personal. Wasn't it Charles who should have been the shoulder for Percy, not the other way around? When Percy lay in bed after their phone calls, he replayed them in his mind, his thoughts snagging on bits of marginalia that Charles somehow knew about the family. He trembled a little and pulled the covers up more tightly around himself on those nights. It did not matter now, he told himself, it didn't matter after all this. Then one day, when Charles started talking about Percy's son's career, Percy flat-out asked him.

"How did you know that my son got promoted to sales manager last year?"

The other end of the line stayed silent until Charles finally said, "Someone at the office said something."

"Sure," Percy said. He had not told anyone at the office anything.

After that day, the calls stopped.

Percy sped south on Highway 52. He was driving faster than he should have been, but he did not care. He felt light and dizzy like one of those snowflakes, the car too hot, the windshield wipers too slow. When he finally got to Rochester, he found Emily's house easily enough. It was on a corner lot at the edge of town, and there was a field next to it. The field looked strange—even in the dark—and it reminded him of the end of the world somehow, as though if he were to step into it, he would never find his way back again. He felt jumpy, afraid of the dark, and so he pulled into the driveway instead of parking on the street. It was hard to make out the details of the house in the dark, but he could tell it was old and white, the front porch peeling and starting to sag. The porch light was off, and he imagined the old woman inside sleeping like the dead, his whole trip wasted. But when he put his hand up to knock, she pulled the door open before his knuckles graced the wood.

"You made good time, kid," she said and then turned around, the open door a gesture to follow. "You want a cup of coffee?" she asked over her shoulder.

"Sure, Emily," he replied, distracted by seeing so viscerally someone else's life. He walked through the living room, the threadbare couch and chairs littered with fabric scraps. In the corner was a large wooden table with a white Singer perched on it. A piece of plaid fabric was still trapped under the presser foot.

The kitchen was grimly papered, the floor covered with peeling linoleum. The sink was ceramic, and the faucet dripped. Emily took down two old mugs, filling one labeled "Escape to Wisconsin" with coffee and handing it to him.

"I don't have cream or sugar, so don't ask, kid."

"That's fine," he said although he preferred his coffee tan and sweet. He sipped it slowly. It was lukewarm and bitter, but still he went back to the brim of the cup again. "I don't have a lot of time," he lied.

"Time schmime. Everyone rushes too much. Tell me about this Bow-neeta. She must be pretty special if you wanted to rush down here at night like this."

He did not know where to begin. How do you describe a whole person? Especially one who no longer talks or gestures or touches you.

"She's a good woman," he said.

"That's it? What does she do for work? You have kids? I assume she's a good cook."

He answered Emily question by question. As he talked, he felt like Bonnie was right there in the room with them, sipping a cup of that terrible coffee, looking pleased at his descriptions. "We have two children. Both grown." *Tell her their names, Percy,* he imagined Bonnie saying. "Samantha and Luke." *Tell her about my potpies.* "She does like to cook. She makes potpies—all from scratch. Big chunks of chicken and potatoes. Best thing in the world." *Tell her about my pancakes, Percy.* "On Sunday mornings, she makes blueberry pancakes better than any diner you've ever been to. She's something, all right." She had been something, all right, he thought.

"Well you sure are a lucky man. It's not easy to find someone you love, let alone someone you can stand to live with."

Percy looked down at the table, at the nicks and gouges in the wood. Nothing stayed perfect forever, but it still functioned. It was still of use. He imagined Charles again—Charles's large knuckles littered with dark hair, which only made him seem more virile. He had only been to Charles's house a couple times, but it was the type of house in which everything looked new. The doors shut soundlessly and tightly. The streams coming from the faucets were full and focused. The toilets did not run. It was not the house that Percy lived in. It was not the house that Bonnie had lived in. Their house had what Bonnie referred to as "character," which was what she said anytime something went wrong. *This house has a lot of character,* she would say and then walk away while Percy was still talking about how he would fix what had broken. Now when he thought of her face and tone, it was like looking at the same intersection from a different angle, and he knew he had let her down— more than just once.

"You got something on your mind, kid?"

"I just hope I made her happy—happy overall."

"Made? You better hope you *make* her happy."

"Make—right. I hope I *make* her happy."

"How couldn't you? You're here, aren't you?"

"Seems like a little thing."

"Don't make it smaller than it is, kid. She's going to wake up and sing your praises. Just you wait. I have something else—hold on." She left the room and returned with a pair of flowered gardening gloves. "Does she like to garden, too? I've started making these gloves. I could make them to match one of the aprons."

"No, she isn't much for gardening or anything outdoorsy."

"Hang on then. I got something else."

Bonnie had hated anything to do with yard work. The only thing she did was plant a row of marigolds along the front of the house in the spring, attacking the small task with efficiency and loathing. That is what bothered him most about what had happened. It was a combination of everything she hated—yard work and disrepair. Now, from the other side of the intersection, he could see how angry she had been when he had forgotten to fix the riding mower. At the kitchen table in the silence in which Bonnie was still alive, the snow melted. The overhead kitchen light became the sun. The coffee smelled like dirt and grass. The linoleum gave and buckled into lawn. He was coming home on a normal Tuesday after a normal day at work. He got out of the car and walked around the house to go through the side door. But before he got to it, he saw her lying on the ground under the apple tree, the push mower beside her. He could feel her name come up in his throat, *Bonnie, Bonnie.* He could feel his briefcase slip from his hands, the slip of his loafers on the grass, and the tug of his necktie as he burst into a run. *Bonnie, answer me!* He had simply not realized he had forgotten to fix the mower, simply not realized how upset Bonnie was with him over it, simply not realized she would take the job upon herself, a job too strenuous for her to handle. And neither one of them could have predicted that her heart was getting ready to explode, that it was just waiting for the perfect summer day to detonate. He could feel himself collapse, kneeling in the grass, his tie dangling in her face. *Bonnie! Bonita!* He could feel his hands on her shoulders, her small shoulders, as he grasped them and shook her, trying to cajole her eyes into unlocking. He could hear a neighbor's lawn mower whirring in the distance, a neighbor like Charles who never would have forgotten his duties as a husband. He could feel himself laying her shoulders down, then turning over and lying next to her, looking up into the hot sun. He could feel himself reach over to hold his dead wife's hand, as faceless names flashed before his eyes, names on paperwork he had processed over the years, names whose claims he had denied.

Emily walked back in the room, her footfalls calling Percy forth from memory. She was wearing a peculiar smile and holding another apron in her hands, but this one was different—tan, unembellished, with large pockets, an apron Bonita now six months dead would never have glanced at twice.

"This one," Emily said. "This one?" she asked.

NOBODY MOVES IN WINTER
For Tom and Brad

"Nobody moves in winter," Nathan says. He is with Michael and they are driving down Nicollet Avenue. It has been snowing the entire day, and the centerline of the road is becoming obscured. On the side streets, cars get stuck. People slip. Tires spin. People fall. Still Michael insists they drive to Northeast to see a house he wants them to buy. "Nobody."

"Northeast isn't another planet. It's not that far," Michael says.

"Are you going to pack?" Nathan says. "Are you going to load up the U-Haul and drive it? Because I am not. I will not drive a godforsaken truck all the way through downtown and over there to old town." He gestures vaguely across the river.

"Jesus," Michael says, tapping his breaks. A car in front of them fishtails as it turns off onto 28th Street. "It isn't like it was when you were a kid. "

"You weren't called 'fag' fifty times a day by Polish Catholic brats."

"You were?"

"You know that. My parents sentenced me to a Catholic school and I was obviously, well—you know—*me*. Do the math, Michael."

"It's different now, you know that. Half of it's an arts district. We have been to Art-a-Whirl."

"Not where you want to move us—all the way by the railyard. It's almost Columbia Heights, almost the suburbs, Michael. *The suburbs.* You know we'll be the neighborhood gays. Do you want to be the neighborhood gays?"

"Cookie, you're exaggerating. This is Minneapolis. I saw R.T. Rybek at a *Miss Richfield 1981* show. Even the mayor is gay-friendly. Besides, moving in winter isn't that big of a deal. We've made enough this year to hire someone to do it for us. They come in, haul out the boxes, and drive the truck, the whole thing. We get hammered off Tempranillo and put away our stuff."

Nathan looks out the car's window. He is still wearing his Monroe wig, red lipstick, and blue knee-length angora dress from the show he just performed; in the window, his silver eye makeup catches the light and sparkles. He poses for a second, studying his reflection. When he relaxes his face, he notices that fog is beginning to collect at the corner of the window near the side mirror. He takes the tip of his forefinger, red nail polish slightly chipped, and draws a small heart in the condensation. The heart travels along Nicollet, through Whittier, and soon will travel to Uptown, where he and Michael have spent the entire five years of their relationship. "I am an Uptown girl," he says.

"Uptown wasn't always 'Uptown,' you know."

"It's always been Uptown for us."

To Nathan, the situation is more complex: once you move away from somewhere, you don't go back. He had been defined by Northeast once in another life, a life he happily watched expire. After high school, he moved to New York, reinvented himself in Chelsea, and then come back to Minneapolis as Queen Paige Turner.

"Northeast isn't the Northeast you remember. Nothing is going to change other than our zip code," Michael says.

"But I have my places. I have my people at those places. I have the girls at Ragstock. I have the trailer-trash lady at Bruegger's. I would even miss that old black guy in a wheelchair who begs outside of Victoria's Secret."

"They won't go away. They'll be right there when you want to see them. And you'll have new people and new places."

Now Pancho Villa, the Mexican Restaurant they always go to on their birthdays, is in the center of the heart. Nathan's last birthday was his thirtieth, and to celebrate, he staged a special show at the Gay 90's. He had a facial beforehand and bought new gold platform high heels and a new white dress. He performed a classic ABBA song, "Dancing Queen," having choreographed a new performance, a performance he felt showcased how far he had come as a queen. His lips, lined and painted, synced perfectly with each word; his narrow hips, sheathed in a flattering cut, pushed against the air to either side of him. He drifted off into the lights, his body once a concubine to the music, now married to it. In his mind, he was in a large performance hall. There were tiers of people to see him, tiers of people who adored him. He was beautiful—his legs shapely, his chest as smooth as it had been when he was just twenty years old. He performed from an idyllic little snow globe of which he was the center, a calf jutting out from the slit in his skirt. At the end of the performance, Michael and the others—people he did not even know—threw roses for him. *They are throwing roses just for me*, he thought. When he looked down and saw the flowers gathered at the toes of his platforms, he thought he should be crying. *They are finally doing it*, he thought. *Finally*. But the tears would not come, so he simply gathered the roses until his arms were full and left the bar, feeling he had lost something.

"It isn't just my people."

"Then *what?*"

At the corner of Franklin and Nicollet, Michael turns on the blinker and its clicking fills the car. Nathan switches on the radio, which is set to a station only playing Christmas music. "Holy Mary, Mother of God," he says, "really?"

"Nostalgia," Michael says, staring off the way of the blinker.

"I forget that about you sometimes." Nathan often takes Michael's habit of nostalgia for granted—the old afghans his grandmother made spread on the back of their couch, the wineglasses from his parents' wedding in their hutch. It is easy for Nathan to forget because he is not nostalgic in the same way, not for family. Nostalgia, he has often told himself, can be dangerous.

They drive down Franklin Avenue until they hit Hennepin. They park by what used to be Birchwood Pharmacy and then start walking toward Lowry Hill Liquors, Michael taking Nathan's elbow and putting an arm on the small of his back to lead him safely into the store.

"Everything would feel so far away if we were tucked back there like that."

"We'd find a new liquor store." Michael holds the door open for him. "Ladies first," he says.

Once inside the store, they roam into different territories, Michael into the reds, Nathan into the whites and champagnes. Nathan looks up occasionally and sees Michael's back turned towards him, and he wonders at that moment what it is that Michael is thinking. Just for once he wants to be a small gear inside of Michael; just for once he wants to turn and grind with Michael's every movement, but not to understand Michael—so that Michael will understand him.

"Miss Paige Turner," the clerk, a young blond man says. "How was the show tonight?"

Nathan raises his chin and gently pats the back of his wig, "Simply wonderful. Great crowd." Then he turns and looks at Michael, the affectation gone. "See?" he says.

Michael rolls his eyes. "Touché."

Once they are both back in the car, heated seats turned to maximum, Michael says, "There's no harm in just looking at it. C'mon, cookie."

To destroy the heart, Nathan uses the same forefinger he used to draw it. "OK dokey," he says, donning a heavy Minnesotan accent. "Whatever you say, dear. You are the boss, after all."

"That's more like it," Michael taps Nathan's knee twice and winks.

Hennepin Avenue is alight with marquee and headlamp, populated by car and pedestrian, both moving slowly through the heavy mess. Windshield wipers flap. Heads shake off snow. The show goes on.

"We wouldn't be that much further from downtown."

"Farther."

"Farther. Would that kill you?"

The car is becoming over warm. Nathan's feet begin to burn, but he says nothing, figuring it is better to save the heat for when they have to trek into the cold dark of Northeast, the back-aways part in which Michael has found the three-bedroom ranch style with a fully finished basement. "We could put a bar and a runway in or a small stage," Michael had whispered in Nathan's ear, his hand stroking the soft skin on the underside of Nathan's arm.

"But then we won't leave the house," Nathan said.

"So? I want us to make a life together. You and me. I want us to be a family."

Those words had stirred Nathan. It was everything he knew Michael wanted, but hearing it aloud scared him shitless. Families were not formal to him; *real* families were pieced-together things, leftovers. He had always been a leftover, the strained relationship he had with his loose-knit family completely disintegrating when he came back from New York as Paige Turner. For five years, he and Michael had been a pieced-together family, and now Michael was ready to change that, to sew what had been pieced together. When he thought about it, he felt as he had when those roses were at his feet.

The car lumbers over the Hennepin Avenue Bridge, traffic diffusing as they travel away from the lights of downtown. Nathan turns his head so that he can see the cityscape behind him. It was always more beautiful the farther you were from it, the sky all mauve with snow, the whole thing silenced by geometry and ice.

Once they cross the bridge and turn onto University Avenue, Nathan gets the same funny feeling he always does. An entirely different city lies before him. Grainy and dimmer, this other city contains the negatives of memories he had thrown in a trash can in New York the day he arrived there. He releases a wealth of air from his lungs, and Michael turns his head sharply.

"Cookie?"

"Nothing. I'm fine. Don't worry about me."

"It's OK, you know," he says, "to want something and be scared at the same time."

"Is there a word for that?"

"Indecision."

But that doesn't seem like the right word to Nathan; it seems horribly inaccurate for what he feels.

Michael's car crawls onto Main Street Northeast. The snow is dense: when he turns the car, the whole front end quivers. Dark surrounds them; the railyard looms, utilitarian, industrial, vacant. The streets are nearly empty.

It all feels so final.

"I think it's at the end of the block."

Before they reach the end of the block, they see a small car struggling in the snow. Michael stops behind it, and they watch as the driver tries to rock the car back and forth to get out of the rut that worsens with each acceleration.

"I should help him," Michael says.

"Just give him some time. He'll get it."

"He needs help."

"He probably lives in the neighborhood. Let's just go around him."

"Would you leave me stuck?"

To Nathan, there is a certain problem with getting into the snow, the silly humiliation of slipping around, the way snow burns skin as it fills shoes or boots. He is used to carrying himself with grace.

Michael opens his door. "I'm going to ask if he wants help," he says.

Nathan watches Michael trudge to the car and knock on the driver's side window. Michael shakes hands with the man in the car. Then he gestures for Nathan to come over. Nathan puts his hands in the air, and Michael gestures for him to roll down his window.

"Boots are in the back of the car," he calls. Nathan shoots him a look of disbelief, and Michael beckons again. "Put them on and come help me," he says. "And grab the shovel!"

Nathan turns around and sure enough, an old black pair of winter boots is in the back of the car, a symptom of the practical side of Michael's nostalgia. *It's better to be safe than sorry*, Michael's mother had said, handing over an emergency kit for Michael's car complete with matches, a blanket, granola bars, and a small red shovel. Nathan reaches in the back seat, his dress shifting and riding up, and pulls the boots and shovel up front. Carefully, he takes off his platforms and works the boots on over his nylons, struggling to get them on in the tight space of the car's front seat. When he opens the door and steps out into the snow, he can only imagine how ridiculous he must look, his hair, makeup, dress and coat all lovely, then the black, clunky, wool-lined boots sticking out oddly below. Nathan trudges towards Michael in the boots and then hands him the shovel. The driver puts his hand out, not an ounce of question on his face. "Name's Walter. Got myself stuck." Walter laughs and then turns away as a figure moves behind the lighted window of a ranch-style on the corner. The light in the front room switches off and a light in another room switches on a second later.

There is something comforting about it.

"Is it—," Nathan starts.

"It is," Michael says, smiling. "He'll steer. We're going to push."

Nathan nods. They get behind the car, and dig their heels in, pushing as hard as they can. The car lurches then recedes, Nathan's wig beginning to slip with the exertion.

"C'mon," Michael says, "Push."

"I am," Nathan says, pausing to adjust his wig.

"Like you mean it."

As Nathan resumes pushing, he has the urge to stop, to let the car stay stuck in that dirty, snowy track. He thinks of the rehearsals before the roses; the cold apartments with leaking faucets, running toilets, but beautiful woodwork; he and Michael's courtship—all the things his life has been crafted from over the past several years. He squints into the wind and blowing snow. He holds his breath as he and Michael push the car forward and then releases it as the car rocks back. They repeat these motions, Nathan sweating and cursing softly. But when the car finally breaks free leaving empty ruts in the snow, he is filled with an unexpected giddiness, as though he could laugh.

Walter waves, and Nathan and Michael wave back. As the car's taillights fade, Nathan turns toward the house on the corner and Michael comes to his side. Nathan reaches for Michael's hand, squeezing it twice, as Michael bends over and picks up the shovel. He plants the handle firmly in the snow and perches his hand on the red plastic blade. Then they simply stand there for a moment shoulder-to-shoulder in the small vineyard of light from the ranch-style, filled with the peculiar silence of snow.

THE PAPER AIRPLANE

I wake up early, too early, and by 8 a.m., I'm already starving. The icebox is full of leftovers, so many I don't know what's good or bad anymore, but I don't want to throw anything out, so I start shuffling through and soon my hands are full. Then the table is full, the door to the icebox is hanging open, and I'm in the middle of all these plastic-wrapped bowls and glass containers. It's a goddamn mess. Penny used to be the one to clean out the refrigerator. Even though she's been gone for a couple months, I still can't keep it cleaned out like she did. I leave the food where it sits because I don't want to waste anything, but my head isn't clear when I'm so hungry. So I walk to 28th and Nicollet, to the Mexican bakery, and I get a couple pieces of chocolate cake with thick chocolate frosting and start eating them standing right in the middle of all those leftovers.

While I'm eating, I start thinking about Penny's hair. It was dark brown, but in the summer, the sun got in it and all the tips turned lighter, almost red. That's when her name really fit her: Penny. When I start thinking about her hair I can see her plain as day, and then I start thinking about all those other things that I liked about her, too, like her ankles. They were thin, but they didn't look weak. Just slim, you could say. And the inside of her thighs, the little rolls she called fat and hated—they were soft and I loved them. She hated a lot of things about herself—things no one could possibly see but her. She'd be sitting there quiet, and then all the sudden she'd say something like, "I hate my teeth," or, "I hate my nose." Then she'd go back to being quiet. But every once in a while I'd home come and she would be crying. Sometimes it was because she said she felt old. I laughed at her—she wasn't much over thirty. She'd get even madder then. It's hard to love a beautiful woman who's aging. They can never see that they'll be beautiful for the rest of their lives. I didn't try to reason with her much after the first time. I'd just rub her hair until she calmed down and wipe the little tears off her cheeks. She was as fragile as a little glass figurine when she got upset.

The cake is good and rich. I finish it standing there in the kitchen. No sense in saving it when I'm trying to clean things out anyway. Penny, when she cleaned the icebox, threw out leftovers just like a woman—quick, on impulse, before she even knew they were bad. "Waste not, want not," I'd tell her, just like my grandfather, who lived through the Great Depression, used to say to me when I'd try to throw away the crusts of my bread. "The point is we'll never starve if we don't waste," I told her. She glared at me every time I said it and told me I sounded like I belonged to a different century.

"I'm not a waster. You're just goddamn stingy," she said.

I said she took too much for granted. But it wasn't like that all the time. Those times were when we were tired, sick of our jobs, when we hadn't touched each other all week.

I clear my throat and try to concentrate on the leftovers getting set to rot on the table. I start going through them, smelling them, and checking for the start of mold. I throw out some deli potato salad, sour milk, and moldy spaghetti sauce. I should have eaten the leftovers right away instead of making something else. Sometimes you just don't think about things like that. You just think about what you want right then because you're hungry and you don't care about what will happen after you eat. It's like going grocery shopping on an empty stomach. You take whatever you can get your hands on. Penny was good like that. She always ate before she went grocery shopping. I eat a chicken leg I know is from three days ago. It's good, but I'm still hungry, so I eat a small bowl of leftover instant mashed potatoes and finish off a container of cottage cheese.

My house, which was our house for the year Penny lived with me, is on a corner lot. If you were to pinpoint it on a grid, it's between Lake Street and Nicollet Avenue. The annual neighborhood block parties now include tamales and black beans and rice, which, as I told Penny, is fine because those people know about not wasting. I respect people who know not to waste things. It doesn't matter if they're from Mexico or Africa or goddamn Abu Dhabi. At the parties, those Mexicans always seemed so happy. The families were standing there smiling and joking, and then up walked Penny and me. Sometimes we were the only white people there. Sometimes we were holding hands and sometimes we weren't. Maybe it was a bad day and we didn't look like we were in love. But once we were there with all those people and we all shared food and made jokes, trying to understand each other, Penny would start rubbing the back of my neck and soon I would put my arm around her. We always felt better after those parties, even if that feeling wasn't going to last.

I'm moving onto the door now. It's full of condiments. I don't know what's good anymore or what's bad. Turns out there's a jar of mayonnaise set to expire tomorrow, so I pitch it into the garbage can. The roasted turkey meat will go soon too, so I make a half of a sandwich, and eat it up because I'm still hungry and I don't want to waste a thing. Some people feel bad about eating a lot at one time, but I don't feel bad about it because this is what I need to do right now and you can't pass judgments on time when you're in it. Which gets me to wondering if Penny had been happy with me. Now that she's gone, I suppose I was happy with Penny. I can't speak for her, except to say that sometimes she hugged me once and then hugged me tighter. In the mornings, she'd wake up before me and when she got out of bed, she'd squeeze my foot, always my right foot, and I pretended to sleep through it, smiling into the pillow. Then I thought she must have been happy. Those were the good times, when I lay in bed listening to her downstairs working in the kitchen. She would turn the radio on and occasionally I could hear her laugh or sing depending on what station she was listening to. I would lay there for a long time after I woke up, just listening to her. That was all before last summer.

Last summer only had a couple lightning storms. I remember the first one best. Penny sat out on the front porch in my grandmother's wooden rocker with her knees against her chest. I was in the kitchen, and I watched her sitting there quiet, watching the storm. When the first growl of thunder came, I started thinking that Penny had a whole life outside me and before me, too. It made me uncomfortable, and I knew I would end up picking at it. I always picked at her and I still don't know why I did it. After the storm, she came inside. We were drinking beer, and I asked her about her last boyfriend who lived in Colorado, why she left him and came back here. I remember she cleared her throat, brushed her hair out of her eyes, but she didn't start talking right away. That bothered me. I started eating popcorn by the handful, washing it down with beer. She told me about the time he took her hiking up the side of a mountain. On the way down, he went first, behind her, and made it easy enough to a ledge, but she had a hard time getting her footing, and before she knew it, her feet weren't on any ground at all. He had his arms tight around her waist, holding her up on the side of that mountain. She didn't sleep that night because she couldn't think about anything else. When she told me the story, she said, "I loved him so much I knew I had to leave right then because all I could imagine was him letting me fall." The next morning she left while he was still sleeping.

"Just like that?" I asked. "You left him that easy?"

"You stay too long, start asking too many questions and things get messy," she said. "I don't like messes."

"You still love him."

"Of course not," she said, but she didn't look at me while she said it and then she got up from the table and went to bed.

I didn't sleep much the night after she told me. I felt like I did when I couldn't sleep as a kid, just lying there staring at the night-light, listening to the old house creak. I knew the score with Penny: there are people you love more than others. Penny loved that man in Colorado more than she loved me. I suppose I realized it because of how she told that story. She would have never said anything like that, of course; she didn't talk a lot, not like most women. Not like my mother. I started thinking of something that my mom said a few months before my parents got divorced. "Your heart can be in a lot of places at once," she said. "It can be split down the middle and you can keep half of that old thing at home and the other half can be across town." I was angry with her when she first said it because I figured—even then—but after Penny's story, I understood, and then I took my mom's advice. It was always Penny that I loved—even when half my heart was across town.

The garbage is just about full now, even after I've pushed it down. The thermostat is on the wall just above it, and I turn it down a degree so that it's set at sixty. I keep my thermostat low in the winter, low as possible, and Penny used to complain about it. She hated the cold, and sometimes I wonder if that's why she left. I never gave in when she complained that the house was cold. I realize it now. I'll never know for sure if that's why or if she found out about my heart and the way it was. On good days, I think Penny left me because Minnesota was just too cold. But on bad days, I think she thought I was just another part of Minnesota, of the North, of the cold. Then I get to wondering if she's right, and so I touch my arm, my cheek, and I feel just like always, so I must not be so bad after all.

I throw out a bottle of expired salad dressing and some eggs, and then take the garbage out. On the way, I get the newspaper off the doorstep. Back inside, I skip to the flyer in the middle, and her name is all over it. Rainbow is having a "Buy-One-Get-One-For-A-Penny-Sale." Seeing her name in newsprint reminds me that she is out there somewhere living her life. Her life hasn't stopped. It's just kept going and going on in a different house, maybe a different town, and maybe she's had a different lover—maybe even that man in Colorado. I set the paper down on the table, which is finally empty.

Now there's hardly any food in the house at all. I open the door and close it, and then open the door and close it again. Broccoli and carrots. A chicken leg. I heat it all up and eat it together and then there is really nothing left. Not even a can of soup because today is my shopping day. I pick up the Rainbow flier again to see what's on sale, but I stop every time I get to Penny's name. I can't stop looking at her name and as I stare at it, I get hungrier and hungrier, and I tear into the icebox again, but there isn't a damn thing left except for condiments, and those won't do. There's flour, sugar, and some other ingredients in the cupboards, but I don't know what to do with those. Penny was the one who did all that.

On Sundays she always made waffles. It was on a Sunday that I woke up and she was gone. We hadn't been fighting at all. The only thing I remember out of the ordinary was that the day before someone had called and hung up twice. No voice on the line, just a couple hang-ups. Penny's forehead pinched up after she put the phone down. "You have any idea who'd be calling and hanging up?" she asked. I remember my stomach turning over, but I kissed her and held her. "I'm sure it's nothing." I said, "It's nothing at all." Then I went out to shoot pool with my old best friend Ray, who always told me I was too old to be messing with more than one woman at a time. When I told him about the hang-ups, he shook his head and said it again, but then he just laughed. My jaw got all tight and I could feel my

THE IN-BETWEEN GIRL

In winter, the light in apartments across Minneapolis hardens and shallows—transient pockets of it all but disappear before dinner, leaving base-colored walls dim and nagging. Hallways narrow, the four corners of living rooms and bedrooms reach toward one another until studios, one-bedrooms become cells. How many of these apartments are spread throughout the high-bricked uniformity of Loring Park and Stevens, its low-rent twin? Through Whittier's cut-up mansions and Seward's divvied two-stories? Hundreds of apartments with splintered woodwork and decaying bathrooms, windows that leak in north wind, radiators that whistle but do not work.

These are the in-between places; no one stays in them forever.

Meg tells herself this as she stares at Tom's T-shirt slung over a chair in her kitchen, precisely where he had left it the last time he was at her apartment. The shirt appears bleached despite its shell-pink color. It has achieved fossil status. All she has left now is this one shirt: the name of some Californian beach emblazoned on the front in tourist font with too-bright graphics above and below it. She still wonders why he bothered buying the shirt at all, since while rubbing her breasts one night, he promised to show her California beaches less visited—the "real" beaches—the ones he had been surfing for years. Repeatedly, he claimed knowledge of secret places, and to Midwesterners, California is a land shrouded in lore, and those who ambassador between it and the Midwest are luminous in the minds of the landlocked. Its attraction is its mystery, a frontier calling.

But there is no longer mystery in the shirt for Meg. Right now she detests it. It reminds her of families she photographed at Sears, families who had obviously just come back from vacation, whose faces glowed from the West Coast sun, while she stood pale in the darkness behind the camera and said, "Smile!" or "Digan queso!" when she felt smart. Still she keeps the shirt because it is the only reminder she has of his smell and thus their sex. This winter she will go without, holed up at her in-between place, finishing the work of cleaning out the remnants of Tom. The cloud-streaked sheets had gone first, followed by the towels and the extra toothbrush, but she is still finding strands of his hair and half-moons of his fingernails, which collect in various cracks and corners like mines in abandoned fields. The shirt will be the last thing to go.

The longer she stares at the T-shirt, the more she wants to get out of the house. It is just above zero degrees, but she is out of cigarettes—a strong motivating factor. Plus, now that Tom is gone—he had often hidden hand-

111

written notes in her packs of cigarettes: *Smokers are jokers. Non-smokers make better lovers*—she feels like smoking simply out of revenge.

Turning twenty-nine had only increased her desire to smoke. There was more stress. Life carried a different urgency; the time she spent in between loves, jobs, neighborhoods was more profound: Tom, photography studios, Whittier and Stevens. Each seemingly insignificant gesture she made had the potential to result in dire consequences: spinsterhood, unemployment, a less-safe neighborhood. As she strived to carve out a tolerable life for herself—which is ultimately what she wanted—she increasingly put herself into context, which only made her worry about dying. In her most recent dream, she looked up and out of a casket. The casket was not at her funeral; rather, it was on display in some funeral house showroom. People walked by touching the pale satin coffin lining, surveying the dark, smooth wood finish, using their thumbs and forefingers to touch the fabric of her burial garment, which was made of pastel cotton, as though she needed to be cool and comfortable in the afterlife. Throughout the time the customers shopped, she kept her eyes closed, listening intently as they murmured phrases like "Hmm … soft," or "Too good to be dead in." Then, they moved past her, and when she heard their footsteps recede, she opened her eyes and stared at whatever part of them she could see from her supine position: a wool-suited back or a pair of hands with a gold wedding ring shining on a finger, hands that twisted a Kleenex around and around. The mornings after these dreams, she felt sullen and heavy, cursing the sun if it shone, wishing for drizzle, and expecting *Kind of Blue* to start playing all around her, music written in the blood of breaking hearts.

Tom had always insisted she wear high heels; she had often refused, but before leaving the house today, she puts on patent-leather heels lined with red satin fabric and thin ankle straps. She knows her choice is impractical, but today she wants to be impractical. She wants consistency inside and out, so she puts on the shoes and walks up 24th Street careful and slow, one foot then the next, click and step, the same rhythm she remembers from hearing her mother's shoes on the pavement as her mother walked away.

The city without Tom is far different from the city with Tom. It seems bigger, less navigable. The lights glow more harshly, the busses run more loudly, the cars speed more quickly, and the homeless seem more destitute, like walking ghosts. In the burgeoning darkness, light snowflakes spin and drop, collecting on the toes of her shoes and occasionally melting on her hosed foot. She thinks of nothing and everything at the same time until mid-canter, a bearded stranger in a knit cap interrupts her thoughts. His shadowed body is ominous against the pristine columns of the Minneapolis Institute of Arts.

He should know better, Tom says. *It's too dark to approach strangers.*

"Excuse me, ma'am," he says.

"Yeah," she replies, already walking away.

"Do you believe in the Lord Jesus Christ?"

"Yes. Yes I do," she says, neither hesitating nor making eye contact with him.

"Bless you then, ma'am," he replies, "Bless you," he says again after she has already passed him.

She continues walking toward Hark's, toward cigarettes, thinking about how simple lying had been. She wonders if her life would have been better or easier if she had lied more. *Yes, Tom, I do think trying to start a surf shop here is a good idea.*

A bright green sign reading "EBT ACCEPTED HERE" is backlit by the fluorescent light inside Hark's. Meg remembers that people had figured out how to use their food stamps to buy cigarettes and she sympathizes with them as she pulls open the door. Warmth rushes toward her from the bright and cramped store, its patrons clothed in bulk, shrinking the store's already-cramped interior. She maneuvers past the automatic teller machine and to the back of the store, where neat rows of beverages line coolers. After grabbing a Coke, she fights past a couple wearing matching leather jackets, who in their myopia are kissing in the chip and candy aisle, their hands firmly on each other's backsides. Behind the front counter, cigarettes dressed in their smart packages smile out at her.

Nervously, she grips her checkbook. When Tom left, she made the decision to let things go for a while. "It can all go to hell for a while," she told herself aloud over her final beer one evening. Hell meant not balancing her checking account. Hell meant eating out, eating leftovers, not cleaning. Hell meant she called in sick for work twice in less than one month. Hell meant she started writing checks because of the delay between promise and delivery. She is nearly positive that her account is overdrawn, and payday is not until next week. But checks are small hopes, and she is trying to be hopeful.

A young man who may be Lebanese or Israeli rings up her purchases and smiles at her.

"Can I write my check for twenty dollars over?" she asks.

"Yes—for you—yes," he smiles. "You are our regular customer."

She feels lighter as they make the exchange.

The cold slaps her legs as she exits Hark's. She peels the plastic from her cigarettes and lights one, smoke trailing behind her as though she is her own locomotive heading north. By the time she passes Franklin, darkness has completely fallen though it is still early. She walks toward the heart of Minneapolis—lights slung around the naked branches of the trees illuminate Nicollet Mall, its blacktopped, concrete vein. A howl of loneliness erupts in her belly as she travels closer to its beat.

Near 11th Street, she peers into Brit's Pub. Its windows are alight, and inside the diners are like animated dolls, their movements exaggerated, their laughter prolonged. Tom would have never taken her there; he hated downtown, preferring neighborhoods where culture was standardized, reliable. So tonight, she walks into Brit's to buy a whiskey for warmth.

The bartenders greet her with cordial nods. "Cold out there tonight, huh?" The bartender says as he pours her Bushmills, neat.

"Yes," she says. "I need strength to go on."

"The perfect thing," he says, making eye contact as he pushes the drink toward her.

Her hands are on the twenty, but she does not want to part with it, not if she doesn't have to. "Do you take checks?" she asks.

He nods. "Sure."

"Great. Why don't you give me one more and then I'll close out."

After she finishes her first whiskey, he pours her another and she writes him a check, carefully adding a tip on top of the amount and signing her name. As she hands it over to him, she feels light and good and she starts drinking the second whiskey wishing someone would talk to her but expecting nothing—it is still early. No man has ever spoken to her before midnight at a bar in Minneapolis, though at midnight, booze-hazed, they came out of the woodwork.

As she finishes her drink, a photograph of Queen Elizabeth catches her eye. Decorous and finely suited, the Queen stares out at her, and she thinks back to when she had actually taken photographs because she wanted to, not because she had to. In the one year of college she completed, her black-and-white photographs garnered the attention of a couple professors. *Full of light*, was what they said, *full of so much light*. Tonight she wishes she were on the way to dine with artists, photographers who admired her work. She imagines walking into an upscale restaurant in her patent-leather shoes and black skirt, standing on her good, strong legs, and inside, some well-dressed man would be waiting for her, holding postcards of her photographs. He would greet her with praise, and she would unfurl compliments from his fingers with an admirable measure of grace. Why had she stopped taking pictures? If photographs were the imprint of one moment of time as seen through the human eye, then all she had to say was that she had stopped being able to see. The unseeing had not been dramatic; rather, it had been a tapering in her vision, a narrowing that had occurred as her relationship with Tom grew more serious, and as their love grew something akin to comfort food. She became content and lost the hunger to pursue a vision she had never been able to focus correctly in the first place.

It is just after Christmas and Macy's, only a few blocks away, has sales. She decides to walk around the store just because it is something to do. Outside, the streets are relatively empty; everyone is in the skyway. She lights a cigarette, and looks up at one branch of it, watching people in suits and dresses, jeans and sweatshirts walking in opposite directions talking, laughing, and carrying briefcases. She wonders what it is they are talking about and where they are all going. There are no stones in her heart; there is no pull, and looking at all those people whose trajectories seem simple and true, she feels silly—a small life, a brief life. She lights a cigarette off the one she is smoking and keeps staring. Public spaces like this one were *a real slice of life*, Tom had always said. Once, when a man hassled her for change in the skyway, Tom just stood there and watched, subduing his naturally outgoing personality. *I'm nobody's hero*, he said.

Macy's, with its light-box windows, is ahead of her and she stops out front and studies the inscrutably lipped mannequins. She walks closer to the glass, until her face is just below one of theirs, the one wearing black pants so tight the drop and curve of her legs are visible through the fabric. On top, the mannequin wears a gray cowl-neck sweater that looks warm, and because of the reflection, Meg can almost see the whole thing on herself. She likes the way it looks.

Just inside the door, she stamps her shoes gently on the rug. Christmas music plays though the holiday has passed, and the mannequins on the sales floor are still adorned in red sparkling garb, a graveyard of the season's joy. After a few minutes inside, she becomes over warm, her cheeks pink with the heat. She takes off her jacket and slumps it over her arm. Her nose runs and she wipes it discreetly with her index finger. She walks nonchalantly past the regularly priced items, stopping to rub a few soft fabrics between her fingers before reaching the sale racks. There are so many dresses: party dresses, evening dresses, day dresses. Black dresses with silver beads, thin straps, and long skirts. Satin and taffeta, no cotton. They are dresses that did not find homes for Christmas or for New Year's; they attended no parties, nor did they make any resolutions. They hang silently on the racks, cool and crisp on their hangers, and Meg is overwhelmed with sympathy.

She rifles through the garments, pulling off any that she can imagine on her frame. After she walks all around the rack, she is holding at least ten dresses. The fitting room is nearby and she smiles widely at the clerk who is waiting to count the number of items Meg is holding.

"Great sales right now," Meg says.

"Sure are. I bought this one," the clerk says, holding up one of the dresses.

Once in the dressing room, Meg quickly takes off her clothes, mindful of her stockings, which she pushes carefully down her legs. With each dress she tries on, she sees different pictures of herself: she becomes a writer, an international businesswoman, a college professor, a dancer. She sees herself at parties, holding a gin martini and smoking an expensive cigarette, pontificating to a flock entranced by her diction, her style, her charms. She is the woman on the postcard, the one worthy of being photographed.

Finally, she finds her favorite dress of the group. It is black satin, tea length, and gently hugs her waist and rear end, moving to a soft A-line at the bottom. The straps are thin; the neck is low. She runs a finger along the top of her breasts, pleased with how they look. She puts her shoes back on and examines herself from all angles. Then she takes off the pumps, puts on the stockings, and does the same. The hard light of the dressing room—which makes her skin appear more pale, her dishwater blonde hair, more ashy— softens and she looks sophisticated. She can see herself moving from circle to circle, a sudden moon with the ability to adapt to any orbit. Yes, she can; she can leave planets behind if she wants. She can start taking pictures again, she can stop Tom's voice from entering her thoughts, she can … she can ….

She takes the dress to the register. The same girl working the dressing room is at the till, and she smiles at Meg over the top of the dress.

"Did you see the earrings I'm wearing?" the clerk asks.

"Beautiful," Meg says.

"They are on clearance right now, too."

"Really?"

"I had a woman buy this dress and a pair of them. They looked really great together."

"Where are they?"

The clerk points Meg in the direction of the earrings, and she walks to the department. The light is low and the jewelry sparkles on the racks. She finds the earrings and holds them up to her cheek. They are chandeliers made of black beads whose cut reflects the low light beautifully. There is a matching bracelet, and Meg picks one up and puts it on her wrist.

Next, she finds herself in the fragrance department, where women are eager to hand her cards spritzed with various aromas, each a new breed of flower or musk. She walks through the smells thinking of botanical gardens, hearing her heels click on the tiled floor, the weight of the dress on her arm. Everyone is lovely—the way they are dressed, the way they look at her. Everything is lovely—the way the perfume bottles shine in the light, just like the earrings and bracelet in her hand.

Her cramped apartment and broken radiators now amount to dead leaves underneath a tree: in the spring, they will disappear.

After selecting a floral perfume, she walks back to the smiling clerk in the dress section, who rings her purchases up. Meg fingers her checkbook. She does not care about her checking account, about the bank, about anything but going home with what is in front of her. Her total is $316.83 and in her best handwriting, she writes a check.

The clerk runs it through the verification machine, and they both stand there, waiting. "They're slow sometimes," the clerk says as she sniffs and looks down at the machine.

"I would be anything else," Meg is thinking, "anything else at all."

Sweat begins to collect underneath her armpits. *It's just money,* Tom says. Money is never the problem; the lack of money is.

Then, the machine begins to sound. "There it goes," the clerk says.

Meg smiles as the clerk hands her the bag over the counter. She takes the escalator downstairs and then walks out onto the street feeling light. Yes, lighter as buses and people move by moonlight, by streetlight, and snow falls heavier on the Mall. Each person begins to look like a postcard, and as she moves through them, it is as if the city is a photograph made of many small photographs. She passes the alley between a furniture store and an import store. In that alley, a trumpet-player wearing a coonskin cap stands statuesque over a case lined in funeral silk, playing a note so loud, so perfect it simply sounds like silence.

THE LAST SUPPER

Melanie had been eating just what she liked: mashed potatoes, ice cream, pudding, but her coworkers at Abbott Northwestern, who had taken a sudden interest in her, were always saying, "You need to eat more. You need more iron. You need more protein. You need more fiber." Now, however, she felt they could say nothing because her stomach was gone, rotted away, and she no longer needed to eat. There was no need to put anything in her mouth, no meat or apples or carrots, because there was no place for it to go. She imagined the food floating around her body, fraying chunks of it knocking against her heart, her liver, her kidneys. The thought of it made her sick, and when they told her, "Remember, you're eating for two," she felt light and dizzy like a Mylar balloon. "Congratulations," the balloon said. "It's a girl."

November had been strange, the weather unusually warm for Minneapolis. Most days she left the house wearing not a jacket but a sweatshirt, which now stretched tight over her growing belly. As she walked to catch the 5A, she waded through rivers and pools of crimson and gold, feeling buoyant, light enough to drift like a leaf. She told her husband this when he came home from his job as a carpet cleaner. He looked at her crossly and told her she was silly. This was the word he now used to describe her: silly.

Right before dinner, he launched into a story about how that very morning he had clipped a red-tailed hawk with his work truck. "I didn't even see it," he said. "Just came right up out of the ditch. Really, *it* hit me. No time to stop. They hunt on the side of the 35, you know, perch right up on the light posts, and then swoop down on the sides of the road. It had probably just eaten dinner."

"What happened to it?" Melanie asked.

"I don't know," he said. "I had to keep driving. Couldn't just slam on the brakes to stop with cars behind me. I never—." She stood up to spoon some potatoes on his plate, and he paused, looking up at her. "I'm going to say something before we eat."

"Something," she said.

He shot her a look. "You know," he said, bowing his head. "To God in heaven, we pray. Thank you for this food on the table. Thank you for our health. Thank you for the health of our child who is getting bigger and bigger every day, and with God's will," he paused, his brow wrinkled, "will. In the son's name we pray, amen."

He pulled his head up and looked at Melanie. She tried to conceal her smile, the corners of her mouth pinched; her eyes had been open the whole time. "Eat something," he said.

"I told you I don't have to."

"Well, I'm telling you that you do. For the both of you."

"It doesn't matter anymore, Ted. I told you."

"How can you say that? You're five months along. I don't know what the angle is."

"There isn't any angle. I told you I don't have a stomach and I'm not going to eat anymore. It doesn't matter."

Ted let his fork fall hard on his plate. "I can't take any more of this … this *silliness*. How am I supposed to talk to you?"

"You don't need to talk to me."

"Why the hell would you say that?"

"You don't talk to shadows, do you Ted?"

He cracked a beer and got up from the table. "You're something else. You know that, you're really something else."

Melanie listened to his footsteps fade into the living room and then listened to the television flip on. It would be religion that came blaring out. He had taken to listening to this preacher and that preacher shortly after she got pregnant; or rather, shortly after she told him she wanted an abortion. Her periods stopped coming while she was on the birth control pill, and they had agreed when she went on the pill that they did not want a child.

"We can't afford it," she had said after telling him she was pregnant.

"We can find money," Ted said.

Melanie laughed. "Are you going to ask your mother? Because my parents aren't helping. They can't and you know it."

"She would help us. I know she would …." He looked down, rolling a carrot back and forth between his fingertips.

"You told her."

Ted said nothing.

"You fucking told her, didn't you? Son of a bitch. You had to open your big mouth and tell someone."

"Please, Melanie …." He came to her and held her, confessing at her knees. "I'll do goddamn anything. Just don't get rid of that baby. I won't be able to forgive myself and God won't forgive either one of us." It was a side of him she had never seen before; she froze, rubbed her stomach, imagining familial tableaux.

"Since when does God matter so much to you?"

"It's in the Bible, Melanie."

"Your mom tell you that, too?"

"She's right. She's right about it. You'll never forgive yourself."

120

"I won't, huh? Is it that or that you and your mother will never forgive me?"

"Please, Melanie, please, baby girl," he said, clinging to her. She had looked up into the overhead light in their kitchen then, the one they still did not have the money to replace, and felt as though she were not standing there at all. Rather, she felt as though she were floating above her own life, above them, above the marriage, and now she could do nothing but sit back and watch the scene. She started laughing, the laugh beginning as a small quiver and building until her whole body shook. Then Ted was laughing, too, and they were both shaking until they broke apart, tears running down Melanie's face.

"You're happy now, aren't you baby girl, aren't you? We decided and now you don't have to worry, right baby girl?" Ted said.

Melanie laughed again, amazed at how easily they had stopped moving lockstep. She turned away, wrapping her arms around a body that was now a stranger, a mess of marrow and sinew that she did not recognize and that—most importantly—she was no longer master of.

"Only in Jesus can man find peace!" The televangelist's voice screamed from the living room. Melanie peered around the corner, watching Ted as he leaned toward the television, elbows perched on his knees, hand gripping a warm beer. "Some people say God isn't here. They say things like 'God is what he is,' meaning that God comes and goes as he pleases. I say that God doesn't leave." The preacher's voice climbed to a fevered canter. "God doesn't take time off from work." He paused. "God is always right there." The preacher beat his chest, patting his forehead with an initialed handkerchief. "Always right here for you to call him when you need it."

The crowd yelled out "Amen!" and Melanie thought she saw Ted mouth the words along with them. She turned away and began picking at a paper towel, insistent as prayer, until a mound of papery flakes lay before her. *Amen*, she thought.

When the program ended, Ted turned off the television. She listened carefully to his movements, translating the slightest sounds to actions. In a moment, she knew he would use the toilet and then—then, "Are you coming?" he said.

"I'm coming," she said, slowly pushing herself up from the table.

"You eighty or something?"

"My legs now. It's my legs."

"They sore?"

"I guess you could say that."

"Then let's go to bed." He took her arm and began leading her to their bedroom. He ran his hand down the nape of her neck. "Come on, baby girl," he said. "We turn back the clock tonight, you know. Extra hour."

They drew near the bedroom, which was dark. Only scant patches of light came in from the street. Though deep within herself she knew it did not matter, the darkness frightened her, the door an open mouth, the bits of jagged light, teeth. "I'd feel bad if that hawk is off somewhere dying," she said. "I'd feel really bad for that bird laying there like that. It might have been miserable and nobody would know it," she said, her voice getting higher as they crossed the threshold. "It might have had to lay there trapped. Couldn't get away if it wanted to."

Ted pulled off his clothes until she could just barely see the white of his underwear. He flopped into bed. "You need that extra hour," he said.

He exhaled and turned away from her so that he faced the door; she was on the inside of the room and she turned away from him, staring at what she could still see of the wood paneling. "Spring ahead, fall behind," she said.

"What, baby girl?"

"I said, 'Spring ahead, fall behind.'"

"That's how the saying goes."

"Why do they say 'fall behind'? Doesn't it sound bad?"

"You're thinking too much. Get some rest so the baby can get some rest, too."

"I don't need rest. I don't need anything. I told you. Shadows don't sleep or eat or anything. They just float along. Most of the time you can't see them at all. Now it's going to be completely light when you get up in the mornings. You won't even be able to see me at all."

"You aren't a goddamn shadow, Melanie. You're here in our bed in our house and our baby is inside of you. I don't know why you keep talking this way. If you don't stop it, I'll make you go to the doctor. You won't talk me out of it this time. You'll do exactly what I say."

Melanie kept quiet; it did not matter, but she did not want to push Ted anymore. She did not want to see the doctor. The doctor would tell her that she no longer had a stomach. He would tell her that there was not really a baby inside her, facts she already knew. Then the waiting would just seem longer.

Soon Ted began his measured breath, light and raspy. In the space of being alone while not being alone, her mind drifted. She could see a red-tailed hawk, and then she was in the air, her vision honed to the slightest movement of gray or brown below. The forest by the side of the highway was sparse, carpeted in vibrantly green grass. It was spring, not fall, and the leaves on the trees were the same resonant green. Then as the wind blew and the grass swayed, she saw movement, a small rabbit darted through the strands. Her heartbeat quickened and she swooped down toward it, her talons extended. But before she reached the ground, she was merely watching from above again. Ted's truck appeared in the distance. He was driving, checking the

122

time: "Spring ahead, fall behind," he said. Then she could see the bird, she could see the highway ….

Melanie jerked awake, her fingers unconsciously crossing her chest, her heart palpitating wildly. Certainly, it would be her heart that would fail next, and she was happy for that. She glanced over Ted's sleeping form to check the time, hoping that when the clock struck two and time turned against itself, her body would gain nothing back that it had already lost.

A GOOD FACE

Frank Drozka was the proprietor of a medium-sized liquor store located at the intersection of two streets—one that led north into downtown Minneapolis and one that led east toward the University of Minnesota. He had a hard face, an old European face that rarely softened while he worked or while he was in the company of strangers. His nose was long and straight, the skin reddish and pocked. He wore his gray-streaked hair slicked back, which called attention to his broad forehead. Around his neck hung a gold chain that he constantly fumbled with between his fingers. It caught the morning light and shone a bit as he leaned over the counter and looked out onto Nicollet Avenue. The street was bustling. People crowded around the bus stops smoking cigarettes and looking at their watches. Somali men sat outside the coffee shop in their fine sweaters and jackets. The block radiated with an energy that matched the sharp winter sunlight, and Frank waited for that energy to enter the store. With the number of regular customers he had, customers who *needed* what he sold, it was never long before someone walked through the door.

After nearly fifteen years of running the store, Frank was finally able to move through his daily routines with a contented ennui, a luxury he had not always been afforded. Frank had begun running the store after his grandparents died. He had never wanted the business, but since he had no other skills or schooling, he took it on, rejecting his grandfather's prudence. Soon his expensive Loring Park apartment was furnished lavishly, and he was running the business in the red. As he watched his grandmother's diamond wedding band sail off in the palm of a stranger, he imagined she was standing over him, her mouth agape in horror. He wondered if it had been she all along and not his grandfather who had been the shrewd entrepreneur. Men needed women, he knew, in a way women did not need men. With that image of his grandmother emblazoned in his mind, he began to change, moving into a cheaper apartment, cutting his own salary, and working more hours so he could get by with one fewer part-time employee. After months of care, the business resumed profitability. He was proud of his accomplishment and embarrassed that he felt proud regaining something nearly lost through his own carelessness.

Finally one of his regular customers—Sam, a middle-aged black man who always wore the same camouflaged jacket—came through the door, a burst of cold air following him in.

"Frank! Hey, my man."

Sam took Frank's hand in both of his.

"Sam, how are ya?"

"Thirsty, Frank. I'm thirsty. You still got them big 'ol bottles of Karkov for twelve dollars?"

"We do. But if I sell you that, hell, I won't see you for days."

"That's what I'm saying—neither one of us would have to see the other's ugly face for a while."

Frank laughed. "On the other side of the reds, Sam."

Sam wandered over to the vodka bottles on moveable metal shelves between aisles. Sam was one of the only regulars that Frank talked to. Frank's grandfather would have served Sam with one eyebrow raised as he did all black men and women, but when Frank took over the store, he changed its atmosphere. Frank served his customers uniformly—all of them except Sam. There was something different about Sam. Behind his friendly banter, Frank sensed shadows lingering. Although Sam was never with the regular drunks who milled around the corner of Franklin and Nicollet, sitting at the bus stop and hollering at women or other people passing by, it was clear that he drank every day. He always came in alone, and Frank doubted that a woman waited for him at home.

He came to the register holding a jug of Karkov. "How's business?"

"Well, as long as you keep drinking, it'll be just fine." Sam wore a cap and sunglasses and a night's drinking on his breath.

"You know I'm not going anywhere, man. Now, what do I owe you?"

"Thirteen seventy-two."

"There you go." Sam never complained about the prices, and he never tried to rip off the store like some others did by attempting to pass off small bills as larger ones, yet it didn't seem he had a job since he was always in the store at random hours, buying the cheapest liquor available.

"All right, well, I'm going to go make some screwdrivers and try to forget that it's about to get cold as hell outside. Low pressure system moving in this week."

"Is that right? Damn." Sam was always right about the weather, a reliability Frank appreciated.

"It's going to be nasty. Stay warm, man."

"You, too. See ya." Then Sam walked out the door and down the street, disappearing into a small East African market.

When 5 p.m. arrived and Frank's shift was over, he lingered for a while, letting the store hum around him. He did not know what he would do with himself when he got home. Finally, his stomach growled and he decided to leave.

"I'm taking off," he said to the part-timers who were in the back stocking. "I'll see you guys on Monday. Oh and hey—make sure you watch the dates on those six-packs of pumpkin beer. That didn't sell for shit."

"Sure, Frank, no problem."

"All right, bye guys."

A chorus of good-byes sang behind him. He put on his thick black sweatshirt and pulled up the hood. He headed straight into the wind blowing up the Mall for his two-bedroom apartment, just east of Nicollet Avenue. When he opened the door to his apartment—sparsely furnished, clean and organized—he sighed. It was not a sigh of discontent, but rather of relief that his house was as he had left it. He used the toe of his white tennis shoe to pull off the opposite shoe and then left them side-by-side on the braided rug near the door. He walked across the living room to the window, pausing to adjust the picture of his mother that hung on the wall. He straightened it, backed away to check his work and then tweaked his original straightening. From the window, he could see the 18-G lumbering off the mall and heading toward Grand Avenue; taxis lined up outside the hotels waiting for passengers. It was November and hard cold would soon set in. He stood for a moment in the gray stillness, wishing that the apartment wasn't empty, that perhaps a woman was standing in the kitchen stirring a pot of soup or that perhaps a woman was lounging on the couch reading a newspaper and twirling a strand of her hair. It all seemed impossible somehow because he had never developed a rapport with the opposite sex. He found himself helpless when in the company of women. Beads of sweat would gather at his temples and words would slide around in his palms like fresh fish. The heaviness of his Midwest vowels would disappear, and the sound coming out of his mouth would become unrecognizable. When this other voice hit his ears, an acute loathing rose in him and most often he found himself turning away from the unfinished conversation, feeling the woman's eyes on his back.

He turned from the window and swallowed hard. The changing of the seasons was a source of discomfort. His nerves always began bothering him, and memories long buried turned over, their tarnished faces shining dully in the waning daylight. He needed to get out of the house. The only thing he could think to do was walk to the Hyatt for a thick hamburger and a few glasses of beer.

Outside, he spotted Sam's camouflage jacket near the bus shelter on the corner, which surprised him. He could have walked by unnoticed, but instead he stopped, relieved to see a face whose topography was familiar.

"Hey, Sam," he said.

"Frank, what are you doing? You going to hit the town or what?"

"I was going to get some grub and have a beer at the hotel."

"That's no place to get grub. That's a damn hotel, man."

"The bar in there has good burgers and it's not too expensive." Sam shook his head and laughed a little. The horn of a taxi blared.

"What are you doing? Where's all that vodka I sold you?"

"Drank up. I had company today. A couple old friends in town. They had plans for tonight, though, so I'm on my own again."

The night was getting colder and Minneapolis was buttoning another button; Minneapolis was wrapping a scarf around its neck. Despite his best efforts, the cold was sinking into Frank, too, and its density made him want to talk.

"Hey, you want to get a burger with me?" Frank said. A 17 shuddered past, creating a storm of dried leaves in the gutter.

"Well, I'd like to, but I think I only got a five."

Frank considered the strength of his desire to talk versus the thickness of his wallet. "That's fine. I can get this one. You've spent so much in the store I feel like I owe you."

"Well, thanks. That's real nice of you."

They walked into the restaurant, and Frank rubbed his hands together, and flexed his fingers, exercising the cold from them.

A waitress hurried to their table, pieces of her hair falling loose from the knot behind her head. She flashed a transient smile, mumbled hello, pulled out her pad, and then looked up at them.

"How's your night, honey?" Sam asked. "Looks pretty busy in here."

She smiled as though she were grateful and smoothed pieces of her hair back into place. "It is."

"You deserve some good tips tonight."

"Tell that to the rest of my section, will you?" Her eyes twinkled in conspiracy, and Frank wished he had made them do that.

"You bet, honey."

"Now, what can I get you?"

Frank ordered them burgers and bottles of Bud. When the beer arrived, Frank drank his down quickly and ordered another round before Sam was halfway done. The alcohol crept into his shoulder muscles.

"You off work now? Doing construction or something in the summer?" Frank asked, not wanting Sam to know that he presumed Sam was unemployed.

"Nothing right now."

"What happened?"

"Nothing happened—recently, anyway. I'm on Social Security disability."

"Oh."

"Now you don't have to say 'oh' like that. Last thing I need is to feel pitied. I'm a vet. Vietnam. Used to mean something. I guess I don't know if it does anymore," He paused. "You ever serve?"

"No, I was too young for Vietnam, and I never enlisted or anything."

"Lucky, lucky."

"I know. I am." A mixture of juice and ketchup ran down Frank's chin as he chewed.

"It changes you being over there. A lot of guys don't come back the same."

Frank looked up from his food long enough to see that Sam had stopped eating. He felt frivolous with his mouth full and Sam's jaw still. He swallowed roughly. "Yeah?" was all he could manage.

"Yeah."

"Huh," Frank said, grateful to the waitress—who, thanks to Sam, was especially attentive—for appearing at the side of their table to ask if they would like more beer.

Frank ordered another round for them. When they had each finished their third beer, Frank paid for their meal, and they walked out onto the street.

"Thanks for the food."

"Anytime. What are you going to do now?"

"I don't know. I've got the ants—I'm thirsty. Gotta find something to drink."

Frank was torn between wanting to see where Sam went and how he would satiate himself and the thought of spending the night in his warm apartment listening to the radio and drinking the remainder of a bottle of Black Bush. He imagined the rooms of his apartment without him in them, the way the light would break on the floor and how the neighbors above and below him would sound. Just as he was about to excuse himself and go home, Sam asked.

"You don't want to come with me, do you, Frank?" As he spoke, he tapped his foot and surveyed the street around them, and Frank felt that Sam was ambivalent to his presence, which attracted him even more. "I was thinking of riding over to Lake. Bartenders over there owe me for bouncing the other night."

"I got a car. I can just drive us over there," Frank spit out.

"That's even better. Let's go."

They walked the few blocks to Frank's apartment where his older Chevy sedan was parked out front.

"What are you driving a grandma car for, man?" Sam laughed and Frank, despite himself, laughed, too.

Once in the car, Frank turned on the radio—AM 1130, KFAN—as usual. The men said nothing, falling into the announcer's voice as he talked about the Vikings and their chances to win the game against the Lions on Sunday. The AM sound transformed the car into its own small world, and that world traveled down Lake Street where supermercados and tiendas were backlit and bright with dresses, shoes, and pictures of hot meats, rice, beans, and tortillas. The Lake Street cowboys, stocky under tall hats, rode the concrete on long-toed leather boots. Frank took it all in and it amazed him as it always did. In his city were other cities entirely: a miniature Mexico frozen and transported at least a thousand miles north, a microcosmic East Africa flown across the ocean and dropped on Cedar Avenue. As he drove, Frank turned toward Sam every so often to find him still, his head propped against the window glass.

"Are you falling asleep on me?"

"No, just thinking. I'm always thinking too much."

"All right, just let me know where we're going."

"I'll let you know when we're there."

At Lake and Chicago, Sam sat up. "Take a left."

Frank parallel parked behind a big SUV and they walked into Sonny's Food and Liquor. The bar was cool and dim; on the white brick walls hung posters, the occasional mirror. The place was dressed in music, and the brown tables and vinyl-padded chairs were filled with a variety of people, young and old. No one turned when Frank and Sam walked in, but when Sam worked his way up to the bar, the men on either side greeted him by name.

The woman tending bar served her way down, dealing out bottles and mixers until finally she was standing in front of Sam. She smiled.

"You getting back on that horse, huh, Sam?"

"Never got off that horse."

She looked at one of the men sitting next to Sam.

"That surprise you?" she asked.

"Hell no, that motherfucker got a stomach a steel. These ole guts can't take that no more. Shit."

Sam laughed, "Come on now, Char, you know you like seeing this ol' mug come through that door. I'm better looking than him anyways." He elbowed the man next to him.

Frank stood behind him, waiting. When he saw Sam settle his haunches onto a bar stool, he thought about just going home, fearing that Sam's ambivalence would grow into complete apathy. He could see clearly the bus stop outside of his bedroom window. He could hear the muffled sounds of his refrigerator and the water filling the dishwasher. He began taking preliminary steps backwards when Sam turned around holding two tumblers of whiskey.

"Now she knows how to pour," he said.

"What do I owe you?"

"Nothing—remember I got credit here."

"Thanks."

"No problem," he said holding his glass up and drinking deeply. "Beam's the best cure for the blues. Let's get a table and then I got to hit the head. Oh, hey—you got a buck on you? We need to hear something good on the jukebox."

"Yeah. Here." Frank handed Sam the dollar.

Sam selected a few songs, and then walked to the bathroom. Old music began to play. Frank did not recognize it because he never took the time to pay attention to music. This music caught him though, and it took him a moment to realize why. Then as the vocals began, an image materialized: his mother's hand stretched out to take his, a diamond wedding ring crooked on her ring finger. He thought of his mother less and less the older he got. Still every year when the leaves fell from the trees, she came to him, sepulchral but beautiful, just as he remembered her when he was only seven years old, before she had been too ill to do anything but lie in bed or practice his handwriting with him. What bothered him now was that when he tried to think of her, his memories were more like photographs than videos. He could not remember her voice as she taught him Polish, the language of her dead mother, or the way her hair smelled. His memories had become square images: white handkerchiefs, thin hair, half-eaten meals sitting alone on a plate in the refrigerator for days.

Now, in a frame, he could see his mother in the cold kitchen of their Northeast apartment, and he forced himself to animate her. She was cutting vegetables for their supper and humming along to her radio. Every so often she would sing a word or two, just audibly. The hem of her skirt swayed as she chopped tomatoes and onions. He could almost hear her; he could almost smell her cooking. His eyes began to well up and he took a drink of his whiskey and then put a thumb and forefinger on the bridge of his nose, staving off the flood.

"That's nice, ain't it? Can't get any better than whiskey and the jukebox on Friday night," Sam said when he returned from the bathroom.

Frank nodded, and the men slipped into a comfortable silence as the music and sound of clinking glasses and conversation filled the air. When they had both drained their drinks, Frank went to the bar and ordered another round. As he approached, he watched the bartender rinsing out glasses, shaking the water off them firmly. She mouthed a few words to the jukebox song, and he thought that just maybe he heard her voice above everything. When he leaned in, she looked up and smiled.

"Two more?"

"Yeah."

"You been around here before?" she asked, as she began pouring the drinks. "You one of Sam's old friends?"

"You could say that, I guess," he replied, clearing his throat. "I run Franklin Nicollet Liquors."

"Gotcha. I know that place. Good whiskey selection."

He nodded. "It's all right." He turned his head and fidgeted with his shirt.

"So what kind of trouble you boys into tonight?"

She kept mouthing the words to the song as she waited for his answer and the familiar tightness began in his chest. She was not remarkably beautiful, but Frank liked her immediately. She had a good face. Her hair was pulled back tight and slick, a small black ponytail at the base of her neck. Gold hoops hung from each of her ears. Their glow lit up her deep caramel skin, and they swung when she moved. Her black jeans were too tight, and small rolls of flesh cascaded over the sides of her waistband. Large dense breasts bloomed out of her tight V-neck shirt. He struggled against staring at them, glancing back at Sam.

"We're just having a few drinks tonight, no trouble."

"I hear you. A laid-back boys' night. I'm jealous." She put the drinks on the bar. "Nine-fifty," she said. She brushed off her cheek with the back of her wrist.

Frank paid her, fumbling with the bills. When she took them from him, her fingertip lightly grazed his. Color came to his cheeks and he turned quickly from her, hearing her knock on the bar acknowledging the tip.

He tried to settle back in at the table, but could not help stealing glances at her.

Sam smiled at him. "Something on your mind?"

"What do you mean?"

Sam lifted his low-ball glass off the table and gestured toward the bartender. "Something on your mind?"

"Oh—no. She's nice, that's all."

"Her name's Char. Char's a friend of mine, you know. I could introduce you, if you wanted. She's a good girl. She's all right."

"What would she want with me? She was talking to you when we got here anyway. Why don't you try with her?"

"She deserves better than me." He stared into his glass.

"Why?"

Sam took a deep drink and said nothing.

"Why?" Frank repeated.

"You ever like looking up at the stars?" he said finally.

"Sure, who doesn't?"

"I used to like looking at the stars. When I was little my pop bought me a telescope—just a little cheap thing. I would look at the stars almost every night and the moon, too. Even when it was damn cold, I would be out in the back yard looking up at those stars. When I got older, I decided I would go to college to study the stars. It was slow going because I had to take time off to work and save up. I had to stop and start. Made everything harder." Sam paused and took another drink. When he set his glass down, a shadow came over his face. Frank got nervous then, his hands began to tingle, and the word *duch* appeared in his mind. *Duch*, a Polish word his mother had taught him. *Ghost.*

"Where were you going to school?" Frank asked, trying to make the shadows leave Sam's face, but Sam ignored him and kept talking, wearing the same painted look.

"Number came up when I wasn't enrolled, so I went and did my tour. You get all these ideas when you're over there. All the things you're going to do when you get home. You're going to get married. You're going to go to college and buy a house. Everything's going to be good when you get home. But then you get back and everything is all mixed up and there isn't any goddamn red carpet waiting for you. You don't know what the hell to do with yourself. You start getting them ants. Can't sleep without drinking. Can't sit still long enough to finish school. No one wants to be around you then." His voice trailed off. He made eye contact with Frank again though the shadow remained on his face. "Still have that little telescope. Still use it, too. Damn thing never broke in all these years. Pop would roll over in his grave."

Frank shot the remainder of his whiskey, then went back up to the bar and ordered more for both of them.

"He's got that look on his face, huh?" Char said, her cheeks and lips softening. "He's going to be that Sam tonight then."

Frank walked back to the table. "Drink up, Sam," he said.

Sam shot the liquor, letting a drop roll down his chin. He started speaking again, but this time his speech was fragmented and the shadow on his face deepened so that his whole face seemed to hang, a weathered flag on a windless day. "Don't know how lucky you are. Sitting on a solid business. Reliable business. You could have a nice girl like Char. Could do a lot of things. You're one lucky son of a bitch."

Frank looked down at the floor.

"You know that, Frankie?" he said, his voice whiskey sharp. "You're one real lucky son of a bitch."

But Frank didn't lift his eyes.

"That's what I thought." He started laughing. "No one that's lucky ever knows it until it's too damn late."

They sat in silence until Frank worked up the nerve to look at Sam, whose eyelids had grown heavy. "You want another drink?"

"No thanks. I think I gotta go. I'm not feeling so good anymore. I gotta keep moving."

Then, as easily as he had come into Frank's evening, Sam slid off his stool. He stopped in front of the bar, followed Char to the end of it, where she slipped him a couple small bottles of wine. Sam leaned over and kissed her cheek. He whispered something in her ear, then looked back to Frank and waved. Frank waved, too, trying not to look at Char.

With Sam gone, the bar became a different city. Frank was a mere ambassador with nothing to offer but clean fingernails and silence. It must be time for me to leave, he thought. But when he stood, he realized the extent of his drunkenness. The room wavered. The thought occurred to him to sit belly-up at the bar and watch Char walk back and forth pouring drinks and smiling. *I'm lucky,* he thought. *I'm one lucky son of a bitch.* He sidled in next to two Mexicans.

"Estoy cansado."

"Uno mas, uno mas!"

"Sorry," Frank said, elbowing one of the men. The man smiled and then turned back to his friend.

"Dos Equis? Bud? Que quieres?"

Char returned and nodded at them. "Two Buds, por favor," the man said.

While she was opening the bottles, she looked at Frank. "Getcha somethin'?"

"Another whiskey, please."

"No problem." She poured the drink and set it in front of him. "My name is Char, by the way."

"Frank." He stuck his hand out awkwardly, and she laughed, shaking it.

"Well, Frank, Sam asked me to take good care of you tonight. So, this one's on him. You can thank him next time you go for hamburgers. By the way, how was the weather when you were out there last?"

"Getting cold as hell."

"That's what I thought. I hate this time of year. Only good thing is the first snow and after that, I could do without any of it."

"Yeah. I don't like it much either."

Talking to her was a small thrill, and he was proud of having made her smile just like Sam had made the waitress smile. She turned and walked away to serve another customer, and Frank hung on her every movement.

"You do pretty well in tips on the weekends?" he asked when she came back.

"Not bad. Once they start loosenin' up, they all turn into good tippers." She winked at him.

He looked down at the bar, vaguely aware that he was grinning like a fool. She leaned over and started washing and rinsing glasses in a small sink. Though he wasn't trying, he could see down her shirt, his eyes drawn to the lines of her white bra.

"Yeah I suppose. Or maybe you're just everyone's favorite bartender," he said, surprised the words had come from his mouth.

"I'd like to think that's true." She laughed. "How's business at Franklin Nicollet anyway? I used to stop in there once in a while. I'm almost surprised that I don't recognize you."

"Business is same as always. I've put plenty of people's last dollars in my register."

"Tell me about it." She laughed and her laughter bolstered him.

"As long as there's those kind around—you know, Sam's kind—I'll be in business."

"Sam's kind?" Her face cooled, and she stopped what she had been doing.

"Yeah, Sam's kind," he said, smiling at her.

"Oh, so you know all about it, huh? You're one of those kind. That's funny. 'Cause right about now you don't look much better off than him." She locked her eyes on him, pupils floating just above the rim of her lower lids, then turned away to serve the final drinks of the night. Char's words rang in his ears, and it took a minute for him to comprehend what he had said wrong. *Sam's kind.*

He had meant it though, hadn't he? Weren't he and Sam two separate kinds? *You one lucky son of a bitch.* His stomach sank as she hustled around the bar, singing along with the jukebox, but never stopping to talk to him again. Soon, the lights came up.

"Drink up and get out," the bouncer called. "Drink up and get out."

Still Frank watched Char until finally the bouncer tapped him on the shoulder and told him to leave.

On the street, he angled himself so he could her through the window. Something about the light and the color of her shirt made him want to stand there forever, watching her mouth moving to songs he did not know. For a moment, he thought she saw him there; for just a second she seemed to stare straight at him. He put his palm against the window glass and felt a pulse. He curled his hand into a fist and pounded along with the rhythm. Char paused in the middle of washing a glass; a piece of her hair fell over her right eye. She put the glass down and gestured at him, just a movement—something, like music, he did not understand. He waved his hand again, but she kept cleaning.

He decided to wait; he could wait there on the street and plan what he would say to her. He would tell her that he thought she had a good face. He would tell her he knew he was lucky, that Sam had showed him. He leaned against the wall of the bar, sliding down it until he was sitting on the sidewalk. Though the city lights had dulled them, he could see the stars. As he stared, a voice entered him and he mouthed along with it: *OK, rybko, put your head back and look at the stars.* Wasn't that what his mother had said when she washed his hair in the bathtub? *OK, little fish, put your head back and look at the stars.* Then she poured a pitcher of warm water over his soapy hair. The voice he heard in his mind sounded so clear that for a moment he thought someone might be next to him. He looked to his right and his left, but no one was there. So, he put his head back and listened again. There was nothing distinguishable, just the city ending a long day, just the city trying to fall asleep under this one thick blanket, stretched and pin-holed. He wondered where

135

Sam had gone after leaving Sonny's. Was Sam standing over on Clinton or Third or maybe Blaisdell or Pleasant with his head back naming constellations? Was he thinking of the telescope his father had given him that he had kept all those years? Or maybe he was in Washburn Fair Oaks Park lying still on a bench just looking, finally thinking of nothing at all.

As the minutes ticked by, he knew that Char would not come out to where he was. Though the bar went dark, he sat still and wondered something that for a long time he had tried to stop himself from wondering: would his mother be proud of who he had grown up to be? In Frank's mind, every mother had a heart of hearts. Like a box locked within a safe, she would keep her secret truths hidden there. Frank knew that in his mother's heart of hearts, she would not be proud of him, though she would love him as best she could. Tears welled in his eyes as he let this surface, finally. Sam's mother had a heart of hearts, too. Frank thought of her, wondering what in Sam's face had come from hers. He thought about how scared she must have been while Sam was in Vietnam, how she must have waited by the mailbox, by the telephone, and how she must have held onto every single word Sam dealt her.

When he stood up to go home, Frank decided that Sam's mother must have been proud of him.

THE NEWLYWEDS

The weather is cold, but sunny, and Carl and Linda have been drinking all day. Their morning started with Karkov and orange juice mixed in lowball glasses still filmy from the night before. Linda put on a Jim Croce record and began dancing around the house to "Roller Derby Queen," spilling drops of her drink on the olive shag. The record was one of the few albums that Carl still owned, as he had sold most of his collection when he lost his job at the Ford factory in St. Paul.

"C'mon baby," Linda said, reaching out her hand. "Dance with me! Let's pretend it's our wedding reception."

"I fell in love with a roller derby queen …," Carl sang, taking her outstretched hand into his. They moved in and out from one another, Carl spinning Linda and Linda rolling out from Carl to shake her hips and do the twist.

Only two weeks ago, they wedded at the courthouse with Linda's half-sister Melanie and Carl's old friend Ted, a man he had met during a short stint in the Hennepin County jail for drunk driving, as witnesses. The ceremony was brief and as intimate as possible for having taken place in a courtroom. When it was over, the four drove to the Round Up Beer Hall and drank until they stumbled. They took a cab to Melanie's house, where they spent the first night of their marriage in a twin-sized bed, holding onto each other with ferocity. The next morning, lit with a haze of alcohol and love, they unlocked each other's bodies with movements both spare and deep. When their lovemaking was over, Linda buried her face in Carl's graying chest hair, and he kissed the top of her head, stands of her fine hair sticking to his lips.

They have been celebrating ever since.

Now it is late afternoon, and they are still thirsty. They hop the 21 and head from their apartment at Lake and Chicago to the VFW on Lake and Lyndale. On the bus, Carl puts his arm around Linda and tells her he loves her. Linda leans into him, adjusting her drugstore sunglasses, and sighs contentedly.

"Carl bear, I love you, too," she says, yawning.

Before they have been riding for a full five minutes, her breaths lengthen and fall into rhythm. Carl can feel her body become heavier against his.

"Wake up honey," he says. "Wake up. We're still on the bus."

She stirs and then sits up. "We there?"

"Not yet. But you gotta stay awake until we get there, honey."

"Ten minutes nap, bear. Ten minutes nap." She leans into him again, draping an arm across his lap.

"No, c'mon Linda, get up." He pushes her shoulder gently and she pushes back. "C'mon, get up."

"But, I'm so tired."

"You'll feel better if you sit up."

She stays still.

"Please, honey, sit up for me."

Finally, she sits up and looks out the window.

"That's my girl. That's my honey," he says, "You have to be awake so we can play bingo. We've got to win that jackpot."

It is bingo night, and they both love getting an ice-filled pail of High Life and holding the brightly colored markers in their hands. Up by the caller, free popcorn is hot and fresh. The salt makes the beer go down smoothly and staves off their hunger so they can drink more before eating a full meal. Steve and Jan are normally tending bar and many of the faces are familiar. The whole place is warm and comfortable, a home away from their apartment.

Their stop comes up quickly, and after they get off the bus, Carl nearly trips walking into the bar. Steve looks at him, blank for a second, and then puts two fingers up in a wave. Carl gestures back, his grin wide and wet. Linda spots Sandy, a woman with long black hair and silver bracelets who she knows only from this bar, but who she has always felt a kinship with. She takes Carl's hand and leads him over to Sandy's table. Sandy's hand is wrapped around a glass of water with a crushed lemon slice floating in it.

"Hey guys," she says as they settle in at the table. "You two already been at it today, huh?"

"It's sunny outside," Carl says.

"And we were dancing. Don't forget that we didn't have a real wedding reception. We had to dance this morning."

"And we love each other," he pokes Linda in the ribs, "don't we, honey?"

"Yes, and we're going to make babies."

"Well, you better get moving on that, sister. What are you, thirty-seven or thirty-eight now?" Sandy says. "Those eggs will rot if you don't use them."

"Hey, now …," Linda starts to protest.

"Awww… I'm just kidding, sister."

"Tell him about it. He's got to love me up more often."

"You heard the woman, Carl. And no woman should ever have to ask twice. God only put you on this Earth for one thing and it sure as hell ain't fishing."

"Well, right now God just told me to go get some High Life for my girl. Ladies." He bows deeply toward them and walks to the bar.

138

"Can I have a bucket of beers for me and my bride over there?"

"High Life?"

"Yes, sir."

"Sixteen dollars."

He opens his wallet; he is two dollars short. Everyone around him is paying careful attention to their bingo cards, so he quickly grabs two one-dollar bills that were left on the bar as a tip. Guilt finds him for a split second, but when he sees the bucket of beer, it slips away. The color, the ice, the glass—it is all too beautiful to feel guilty about how he got it. Grinning, he hands the money to Steve, who says nothing when passing over the beer.

Linda waves at him as he approaches the table, her sunglasses sliding down her nose.

"You're still wearing your shades, honey."

"I gotta keep something between them and me," she says.

"Silly little honey." He kisses the top of her head.

They keep talking with Sandy, who sips her water as they drain their beers.

"Here," Sandy says, "take this. Congratulations on gettin' hitched. Play bingo."

"Really?" Linda says, taking off her sunglasses.

"Really. It's only a couple bucks and it's not like I got to get you a wedding gift or anything."

"You're all right, Sandy. You're really all right," Carl says.

"It's only a couple bucks."

Linda reaches across the table to hug her, but knocks over Sandy's glass.

"Whoa, easy cowgirl," Sandy says. "We can just shake on it."

Linda laughs and takes Sandy's hand in both of hers. The women are quiet for a moment. Then Linda puts her sunglasses back on and goes up to get cards and markers for bingo.

During the third game, Sandy's gift grows exponentially when Linda wins the jackpot. She puts her fist in the air when she calls it. The bartender looks at her and she claps her hands together. Carl kisses her on the cheek and Sandy gives her a high-five. Then, Jan comes over to give them a free bucket of beer and a crisp, clean fifty-dollar bill. They break the bill on a thin crust pepperoni pizza that Steve cooks in a small oven behind the bar. He cuts it into squares and Sandy picks at her piece while Carl and Linda devour the rest, burning the roofs of their mouths on the cheese, though they will not know it until they wake in the morning.

They play another couple rounds, but win nothing. Soon their beer is drunk; Sandy leaves, and so finally, Carl and Linda leave, too.

"Here, little honey, put this in your pocket and keep it safe for us, OK?" Carl says, handing her what is left of the fifty.

Outside, daylight is traceless. At the bus stop, Carl rests his chin on top of Linda's chestnut hair. They hold each other tightly and Linda sways her hips back and forth against Carl's pelvis. Between them, the Minneapolis dark and cold has disappeared. Carl puts his hands in Linda's back pockets; he can feel the bills neatly folded inside. He rubs his fingertips up and down the length of them, feeling safe, for now.

They are riding the end of Carl's unemployment checks, and though Linda has hinted around about it, he has avoided finding out just when the checks will stop coming, but he knows they will stop coming too soon. Linda has a bad back and gets some disability benefits, but not enough to support them. Every month, she gives some of the money to her mother, an elderly woman voiceless from cancer, who still inhales cigarettes through the hole in her throat. She does not tell Carl she does this, but since they are married, she figures she will have to because now she and Carl are a family, a tribe onto themselves. They both know that soon one of them will have to take whatever work is to be found: dropping potatoes in grease, guarding merchandise, cleaning hotel rooms. But for now, they are still safe from that life.

At the bus stop, waiting for the 21, they do not think. Carl squeezes Linda's behind, kneading her flesh and kissing her neck. The lighted windows of the 21 take them by surprise, so Carl quickly pulls his hands from Linda's back pockets, and then they both board carefully. Carl uses the last ride on his pass and gets a transfer. Linda digs through her jacket pockets while the bus driver waits. "I know I have it," she says.

"We'll wait right here until you find it," the driver says. "Otherwise, you'll have to find another way home."

The riders stare as she fumbles through her pockets.

"I told you to keep it right here, honey," Carl says, tapping the front breast pocket of her jacket. "I told you to always keep it right there." His tone is gentle. "You have to keep your pass safe."

The driver clears his throat, and exasperated sighs fill the bus.

"I know. I thought I had it."

She unzips her purse, dropping one of its straps. A red wallet, a compact, a tampon fall out. Carl stoops over and begins picking up her things.

"C'mon, little honey," he says. "They're waiting on us."

She dumps what is left of her purse on the empty front seat of the bus, and the pass lands on the blue vinyl. Without saying anything, she turns around and slides it into the reader. The driver pushes a button and her transfer pops up.

"Looks like you got a ride," he says, putting the bus in motion.

The only two empty seats are in the front on opposite sides, so Carl and Linda sit facing one another.

140

"Now take that money from bingo and either put it in your purse or give it to me to put in my wallet, OK, honey? We can't lose that because we're still supposed to meet up with Ted and Mel later."

"OK, OK. Don't talk to me like I'm a kid."

"I know. I'm not, little honey. We just have to make sure we have enough for tonight. I'm cashed out until next week.

Linda leans forward and puts her hands into her back pockets. She takes them out and looks at them, and then puts them back again.

"Well what in the hell?" She says.

"What?"

"I can't find it."

"You can't find it?"

"I thought it was back here." She puts her hand in the back pocket of her jeans, her fingers groping against the denim. "I thought I put that money right there."

"You did. I know you did. I felt it in your back pocket."

"Well what could of happened? I didn't buy anything else after we left the bar."

"Fuck! Damn it, Linda. You were supposed to keep that money safe."

"Don't yell at me. Don't you yell at me. It's gotta be here somewhere."

The other riders look at them too long, turning away politely when they sense they are on the verge of getting caught if not by Carl and Linda, then by each other. Linda continues to search through every pocket in her purse and on her clothing. She pauses for a second and pulls her sunglasses out. Slowly, she slides them on her face.

"Damn it, Linda."

"Don't blame this all on me."

"You're the one who had it, didn't you? So you should know what happened to it."

"I don't know. But don't blame it all on me."

"It was right there. I felt it."

"If you felt it, maybe you took it out of my pockets. Maybe you got it."

"I don't."

"You didn't even look. Why don't you look? Check all your pockets. Even that little one that's just for quarters."

"I'm telling you. I don't have the money."

"Do it anyway."

"Jesus Christ."

He searches his pockets quickly, but thoroughly, all thumbs and digging. He pulls out receipts, lint, and pennies, but no bills.

"You don't have it either," Linda says, simultaneously asking a question and making a statement.

"Shit," he says.

"See? It could of been either one of us. You can't blame it all on me."

"I'm not. I'm sorry, little honey. I just don't like us going around with nothing in my wallet. Makes me feel like nothing."

They are silent for a moment, each watching opposite sides of Lake Street float past.

"I just hate it. Going around with nothing, with an empty wallet. Makes me feel like nothing," Carl repeats.

"Stop it," Linda snaps. And then, more gently, "Maybe Melanie can lend us a twenty."

"I hate borrowing."

"Stop it, bear. Don't talk that way. I've given Mel plenty. And what about Ted? Doesn't Ted still owe you for helping him do drywall? I think he still owes you, bear. He'll be good for at least a $20."

"Yeah, honey. You're right. Ted should be good for a $20. He's got to."

As the bus bounces along, they stare at one another silently across the aisle. Carl smiles at Linda, and then looks at the woman sitting next to her. "Hey—hey, will you switch spots with me? That's my girl you're sitting next to. She's my bride and I want to sit next to my bride."

"Sure, I can switch with you," the woman says.

"Thanks—thank you, ma'am. She's my bride and I just have to sit next to my bride."

Carl and the woman stand. Carl stumbles as the bus comes to an abrupt stop. He grabs the bar above his head for support. When he and the woman are both settled in their new seats, he says, "We were just married, just two weeks ago." He puts his arm out and Linda leans into him, their bodies coming together thoughtlessly.

"You're my bride, aren't you? Just my little bride."

"Yes, bear," she says and the bus bumbles along, causing her breath to slow and lengthen once again. Carl leans his head against the window and closes his eyes, moving his hand gently between her breasts to where he can feel her heart beating.

About the Author

Darci Dawn Schummer, a Wisconsin girl, is the eighth daughter of a firstborn son. Since moving to Minneapolis, Minnesota, and graduating from Hamline University's MFA program, she has published short fiction in places such as *Paper Darts*, *Conclave: A Journal of Character*, *Vita.mn*, *Everyday Fiction*, *Revolver*, *Midwestern Gothic*, and *Open to Interpretation: Intimate Landscape*. This is her first book. Currently, she teaches English at Hennepin Technical College and lives alone in an old Minneapolis upper with her books and records and dresses. You can visit her at www.darcischummer.com.